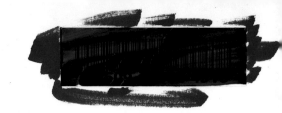

The PRIZE WINNERS of PIEDMONT PLACE

Also by **Bill Doyle**

Attack of the Shark-Headed Zombie
Stampede of the Supermarket Slugs
Invasion of the Junkyard Hog

The PRIZE WINNERS of PIEDMONT PLACE

Book 1

by **Bill Doyle**

illustrated by **Colin Jack**

Random House New York

Text copyright © 2016 by Bill Doyle
Jacket art and interior illustrations copyright © 2016 by Colin Jack

All rights reserved. Published in the United States by
Random House Children's Books, a division of
Penguin Random House LLC, New York.

Random House and the colophon are registered trademarks of
Penguin Random House LLC.

Visit us on the Web! randomhousekids.com

Educators and librarians, for a variety of teaching tools,
visit us at RHTeachersLibrarians.com

Library of Congress Cataloging-in-Publication Data
Names: Doyle, Bill H., author. | Jack, Colin, illustrator.
Title: The Prizewinners of Piedmont Place / by Bill Doyle ;
illustrated by Colin Jack.
Description: First edition. | New York : Random House, [2016] | Summary:
"Eleven-year-old Cal must convince his lovably wacky family to compete in a
contest where the winners are granted twenty minutes to grab anything from
King Wonder's world-famous shop"—Provided by publisher.
Identifiers: LCCN 2015029585 | ISBN 978-0-553-52177-1 (hardback) |
ISBN 978-0-553-52178-8 (hardcover library binding) |
ISBN 978-0-553-52179-5 (ebook) |
Subjects: | CYAC: Family life—Fiction. | Contests—Fiction. | Stores, Retail—
Fiction. | Humorous stories. |
BISAC: JUVENILE FICTION / Humorous Stories. | JUVENILE FICTION /
Family / General (see also headings under Social Issues). | JUVENILE FICTION /
Action & Adventure / General.
Classification: LCC PZ7.D7725 Pr 2016 | DDC [Fic]—dc23
LC record available at http://lccn.loc.gov/2015029585

Printed in the United States of America
10 9 8 7 6 5 4 3 2 1
First Edition

Random House Children's Books supports the First Amendment
and celebrates the right to read.

For the Macatawa crew
and racing backward up the hill
–B.D.

To my lovely wife, Michelle
–C.J.

What's on YOUR wish list?

A go-kart,

a waterslide,

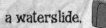

or maybe a robot best friend?

King Wonder wants to grant <u>your</u> wish!

ENTER THE **GREAT GRAB** CONTEST!

You and your family could win a run through
the new WISH SHOPPE superstore in your town.
Grab and keep EVERYTHING you want!

The contest starts Tuesday at exactly 7 PM
on Palmer's Farm in Hawkins, Michigan.

WILL YOU BE THERE?

KING WONDER'S WISH SHOPPE
WISH WELL!

When the pancake hit the fan, Cal Talaska wondered if he'd gone too far.

The pancake was still raw, like watery pizza dough. So when the eleven-year-old tossed it up at the ceiling fan, it exploded. *Splith! Splith! Splith!*

As gooey globs of batter rained down in the kitchen, Cal ducked. But the family dog bounced straight in the air like a mini pony on a trampoline. Butler's long tongue snagged falling pancake drops while his tail whirled like a propeller. Cal's little brother, Bug, tried to reach the batter first as it splattered on the kitchen table and the counters. But the four-year-old was half the size of Butler, and the dog kept beating him to the prize. Finally, they crashed into each other, knocked over a chair, and tumbled to the floor.

A smudge of pancake had dripped onto Butler's back. The dog spun around and around on his side, trying to lick it off his fur. Trapped against Butler's belly, Bug spun with him and giggled hysterically. They were a swirling, slobbering ball of nuttiness. It was exactly the kind of noisy chaos Cal wanted.

Just as he knew she would, their mom pushed open the kitchen's swinging door. "What the cheese is going on?" Mrs. Talaska demanded.

"The Butler did it!" Cal cried.

"Not funny, Cal." Mrs. T. switched off the fan, but not before a glob of pancake flew onto her forehead.

Cal didn't want her to be mad. He pushed back his black hair and put on his most adorable face. "Surprise! I'm cooking pancakes for dinner! In the microwave!"

Mrs. T.'s green eyes softened. "Honey, I was thinking of making baked chicken and a salad." She bent over to untangle Bug and Butler. Bug reached up and dipped his finger in the blob on her forehead.

"Gron't!" Mrs. T. said, saying "Gross!" and "Don't!" at the same time.

Too late. Bug popped his finger in his mouth. His

eyes lit up as he got a taste of the pancake goo. It was like giving a drop of water to a man dying of thirst. He had to have more—and if he didn't get more, a tantrum would be on its way.

Bug was going through a phase. He didn't really talk except to bark with Butler. Mrs. T. said he would grow out of it in a few weeks or so. His tantrums, though, had become epic. When cranky, Bug might dig a hole in the backyard with Butler for hours. Or he might twirl in the kitchen for half an hour until he threw up.

Holy Aristotle, Cal thought. He and his mom shared a look across the room.

"Get your dad and sister in here," Mrs. T. said. "STAT!"

"Dad!" Cal yelled at the top of his lungs. "Imo!"

"Criminy, Cal, that's not what I meant—"

Mr. Talaska burst into the kitchen. He was even taller than Cal's mom, and his broad shoulders barely fit through the door. His glasses were slanted across his face. He turned them diagonally when he wrote music. He said it helped him see the notes better.

"We've got a BTA on our hands," Mrs. T. told him.

At the code for *Bug Tantrum Alert,* Mr. T.'s eyes darted to the door, as if he might run for it.

"No, you don't," Cal's mom commanded. "We need pancakes—"

"—and we need them now!" It was Imo. Cal's nine-year-old sister ran into the kitchen and opened a drawer next to the sink. "Ground Control to family: Why are you just standing there?" Imo said, tucking a whisk and measuring spoons into the pockets of her overalls. "Don't you see what's about to happen?"

Cal did, and he was suddenly nervous. His plan had been to gather his family and eat early. That way, he could get them out the door to a top-secret spot by seven PM. But he was playing a dangerous game. If he didn't get Bug a pancake, they wouldn't be going anywhere but Meltdown Town.

The tiny batch Cal had made in the microwave was useless. They had to start from scratch.

"Talaskas together!" Cal said. "Let's make pancakes!"

Mr. T. manned the griddle as if it were one of his favorite musical instruments. Imo took charge of the kitchen tools. And Mrs. T. looked through her box of recipes until she found just the right one. Cal moved like lightning around the kitchen. He cracked the eggs, gave advice on the right time to flip, and kept everyone on track.

Six minutes later—a Talaska record—the first

pancake hit Bug's plate. Everyone took a seat with a plate of pancakes. The family waited. Bug didn't move. In fact, he looked more ready to blow than ever.

"What's with the look?" Mr. T. asked. "It's perfectly cooked!" He rhymed when he was excited or nervous.

"Oh!" Cal realized what was up. He rushed to the dishwasher and grabbed Butler's dog bowl. He slid a cool pancake into it and put the bowl at Bug's feet. Once Butler had a flapjack, too, Bug grinned . . . and stuffed an entire pancake into his mouth.

"Disgusting," Imo said.

"Better not laugh, Bug," Cal said. Which he knew was the worst thing to say to someone you didn't want to laugh.

Bug's pancake-filled cheeks quivered, ready to explode.

"Stop!" Imo yelled at both Cal and Bug.

"I'm serious, Bug," Cal said. "Don't laugh."

Bug's lips stretched into a smile, and a tiny pancake glob slid out, like air seeping from a balloon that was about to pop.

"Quick!" Cal said. "Distract him. Somebody say something sad!"

"Like what?" his mom asked.

"Homework!" Cal yelled.

Imo looked offended. "That's not sad."

"I don't know what to say, then," Cal said. Actually, though, he did know. This was going just the way he had hoped. "Let's talk about something *not* funny. Say something you want. Mom, you start."

Mrs. T. seemed anxious, watching Bug's mouth like it was a ticking bomb.

"Mom?"

With a distracted shrug, she finally answered, "I want to get in shape."

"How? Specifics, please!" Cal said. More pancake drool slid down Bug's chin. "Like, for instance, *I* want the Wonder World Video Game System—"

"That costs almost eight thousand dollars!" Imo protested.

"Dream big!" Cal said. "Now you guys go, fast!" He pointed to his mom.

"I want a home gym," she said.

"Great," Cal said, and pointed at his dad.

"I want a new piano," Mr. T. said. "No, wait, I want an orchestra!"

"I want a laboratory to make spacecraft," Imo said without hesitating.

Bug mumbled something like *mmmph,* which shot a small spray of pancake juice out of his mouth. Butler barked in agreement. And then the pancake slid down Bug's throat, reminding Cal of a boa constrictor swallowing dinner.

Bug thanked the family with a happy thumbs-up. Everyone breathed easier as Mrs. T. put another pancake on his plate. This time, she cut it up for him.

"Could there be anything better than breakfast for dinner?" Mr. T. mused, sopping up the syrup on his plate with his last forkful.

There might be, Cal thought, glancing at the kitchen clock. But they'd have to hurry if they were going to find out. He needed to get his family to the secret spot in under half an hour.

"Whipped cream might've made it even better," Cal said, knowing this would get his mom thinking about walking.

"True," Mrs. T. said. "But all that extra sweetness would've meant an even longer walk after dinner, and I have so much work to do tonight."

Mrs. T. was always busy. Her job was bringing sports stars to their small town in Michigan. The athletes gave speeches at the auditorium about reaching goals and staying healthy. Cal's mom sometimes laughed that she should practice what they preached. She was always trying new fitness routines. The latest one involved a lot of walking.

That walking could work into Cal's plan. He just needed to plant an idea. "The park, the park, the park," Cal mumbled softly.

"What, Cal?" Mr. T. asked. "Did you say 'the park'?"

"The park?" Cal repeated at full volume, as if his dad had just come up with the best idea. "The park it is! We can all walk with Mom once we're there. Here we go!" He grabbed the family's plates in a big stack and put them in the sink.

Before anyone could protest, Cal rang the small bell they kept on the kitchen counter. The Talaskas rang it when someone had a good idea or wanted to call a family meeting. Once Cal had their attention, he herded everyone toward the back door. His mom went in the other direction, toward the griddle. "I need to clean this—"

Cal gently steered her away. "I'll clean up everything when we get home."

Mrs. T. stopped. "Hold on, mister. What's going on here?"

By offering to do something for nothing, Cal had

gone too far. He needed to tone it down. "I mean . . . ," he said, "I'll clean up for a small fee."

That seemed to satisfy his mom, and they hustled out the door. On the driveway, Bug and Butler were already in the back of the Flying Monkey. That was what the family called their beat-up car. Imo poked at the compact's front-right tire, which had sprung a leak a few days earlier. "The patch I put on is holding up pretty good," she said. "In my opinion, I'm one awesome mechanic. Probably the best in the world, don't you think, Cal?"

Cal bit his tongue. He didn't have time to argue. "That's right!"

Imo frowned. "Why are you agreeing with me?" she asked. "What are you up to, Cal?"

Cal didn't answer. He squeezed into the front with his mom and dad, and Imo got in the back.

"Buckle up, kids," Mrs. T. said as she turned the ignition. Then, as the car wheezed out of the driveway, she added, "Tight."

The Flying Monkey trundled down Piedmont Place. "We Are Family" played on the car's stereo . . . as always. The CD was stuck in the Flying Monkey's old-fashioned CD player and ran on a loop whenever they turned on the car. Imo had offered, and sometimes begged, to get it out, but Mr. and Mrs. T. always shook their heads. "It's our song now," Mrs. T. would explain.

They were driving past Palmer's Farm when they spotted a group of cars and people at the side of the road. Mr. Palmer had rented out space along the road for a giant billboard for the new Wish Shoppe superstore. And the crowd was clustered between the sign and the cornfield.

"What's going on at Palmer's?" Mr. T. asked.

"It looks like a rally or something," Imo said. "The

Donegan Diner's food truck is there. And so is the mayor's motorcycle."

Cal looked at his watch: 6:57. Just in time. "We should check it out," he suggested. "We can walk to the park from here."

They pulled in next to the other cars and piled out of the Flying Monkey. Over the heads of the crowd, they could see a bald man with a megaphone jump up onto a small stage.

"Hello, folks!" the bald man said with a big grin. "I'm Paddy Vance, Vice President of Fun at Wish Shoppe. Welcome to the first stage of our Great Grab Contest!"

The crowd clapped and cheered.

"King Wonder is opening a Wish Shoppe in your town that will have over five acres of amazing products," Mr. Vance announced. "One lucky family will get twenty minutes to run through those acres and grab whatever they want! But let's not get ahead of ourselves. First, families need to pass through today's elimination round!"

"Wow," Cal said to his parents. "Sounds cool, doesn't it? Want to take a closer look?" Without waiting, he squeezed by people toward the front of the group.

"Hold on a second, Cal," Mr. T. said, trying to pull

him back. "I think that's my boss, Mr. Wylot, and his family over there. I don't want to see him right now."

Cal kept leading the Talaskas through the crowd. People shook their hands and patted Butler on the head. A neighbor, Constance MacGuire, reached out to squeeze Mrs. T.'s shoulder. "Good luck!" she said warmly.

"Uh, okay, thanks," Mrs. T. replied, confused. "We're just going for a walk in the park."

"There's a space right here." Cal moved them into an empty slot in a line of other families.

Once they were in place, the Talaskas had a clear view of Mr. Vance.

"Hello to those of you who are just joining us!" Mr. Vance said through the megaphone. "As a child, King Wonder, the founder of Wish Shoppe, was inspired by his pet butterfly. The flapping wings made him want to soar. Today, your challenge is to capture your own butterfly!"

Mr. Vance pointed dramatically to thirteen wooden poles that were lined up along Palmer's cornfield. They were twenty feet high and looked like telephone poles. Each one had a stuffed purple butterfly the size of a toaster stuck on the top and a treasure chest at the bottom.

"Which three families will get the butterfly off their pole first and become finalists in the contest? Let's find out!" Mr. Vance took a breath. "Ready?"

The audience hooted and applauded, some yelling out different family names.

"Why are people cheering?" Imo asked nervously. She looked down at the white line on the grass at her feet. "And what's this?"

"That's a starting line," Cal said. No point in trying to trick anyone anymore.

"Set?" Mr. Vance cried.

"Uh, Cal," Imo said. "Why are we standing at a starting line?"

Cal shrugged. "Because we're about to run a race."

This caught Mrs. T.'s attention. "Wait, what the goat cheese is going on?" she said in a panic.

As if to answer her, Mr. Vance shouted, "Go!"

KA-BLAM! A starter cannon fired. And, just like that, the Talaskas had entered their first contest.

The other families around the Talaskas raced off. Cal sprinted a few steps toward the pole meant for them, but he realized his family wasn't moving. He turned back. "Let's go! Let's go!"

His parents looked more stunned than mad. But not Imo. She was just mad. "I'm not going anywhere with you," she said, driving the heels of her sneakers into the ground. "You tricked us."

"For your own good!" Cal shot back. He glanced over his shoulder. The other families had already reached the poles with the butterflies. "If we win today, we'll be in the running for the Wish Shoppe Great Grab! We'll get whatever we want in the store for free!"

Imo dug her heels deeper and wouldn't budge. "You just want the world's biggest video game."

That's not all, Cal thought. But he said, "Absolutely! And you want stuff, too." Cal turned to the rest of his family. "You said it yourselves. A home gym, an orchestra, a spacecraft laboratory, and . . ." Cal pointed at Bug and Butler. "You two want *mmmph* or whatever." Butler wagged his tail and barked, "Rabbo!"

Mrs. T. lightly tapped Cal's forehead. "We're not puppets," she said. "And you're not a puppet master."

"We'll talk about it at home, pal," Mr. T. said. He didn't like causing a scene. "My boss just heard everything you said, Cal."

Now it was Cal's turn to panic. They couldn't go home and lose this chance! "If I'd asked you, what would you have said?"

"NO!" his family shouted back.

"See? I was right to do what I did!" Cal insisted. "We just have to be one of the first three families to get a butterfly down from a pole. But we need to move now!"

Most of the families had climbed up on the chests at the bottom of their poles. Some tried to shake the butterflies loose, and others tried knocking the poles over with kicks and shoves. Cal spotted his best friend, James, and James's dad climbing their pole. After just a few feet, though, James's hands started slipping and sliding and he dropped onto his dad. They both tumbled onto the grass, laughing.

"Hey!" James yelled, rubbing his hands on the ground. "The poles are covered in slime!"

Other families were finding that out for themselves. People were sliding down the poles all along the field. Getting desperate, a few tried jumping up to grab the butterfly. But it was twenty feet off the ground, so they weren't even close. The football coach from the high school leapt in the air, landed off balance, and slid onto his rear.

"You'll need wings to make that jump, Coach Eaton!" Mrs. Moylan, owner of the Hawkins gas station, shouted from the audience.

The coach chuckled, and the crowd laughed with him. But not Cal. He had his eye on the treasure chests next to the poles. He had a feeling there was something inside those chests that could help with the challenge. But it might already be too late.

"Look at that!" Mr. Vance, the VP of Fun, yelled into

his megaphone. He was watching the Wylots, and soon everyone else was, too. "Have you ever seen anything like it?"

Mr. Wylot was Mr. T.'s boss at the factory, and Leslie Wylot was in Cal's class. But it was the older daughter, dressed in hunting clothes, who had snagged all the attention. Emma Wylot was like a ninja. Somehow, the thirteen-year-old had shinnied up the greased pole, even though it was as slippery as ice. Emma plucked the butterfly off the top. She held it out and, with her legs extended in a straight line, slid down the pole one-handed, like she was a human flag.

Once on the ground, Emma handed the butterfly to her dad. And the family lifted Mr. Wylot into the air, as if he had done all the hard work. He waved at the crowd like a king home from battle.

"We have our first winners! The Wylots!" Mr. Vance shouted. A few people clapped. "And the second family doesn't look far behind!"

It was true. The Rivales, who lived next door to the Talaskas on Piedmont Place, were just inches away from nabbing a butterfly. Mr. and Mrs. Rivale and their identical triplets—three teenage boys—had built a human pyramid that would have wowed the ancient Egyptians. The parents stood next to each other, forming a base. The first triplet stood on their shoulders, with the next triplet on his shoulders and the third on top. Like a circus act, they formed a tower rising twenty feet in the air. A few families stopped what they were doing to stare as the top triplet grabbed the butterfly and slid down his other family members to the ground.

"We have our second family!" Mr. Vance cried. "Who will be the third and last one?"

"We will!" Cal yelled. "Come on, Talaskas!"

Still, his family wouldn't move. Cal couldn't take it anymore. He ran by himself to the chest at the bottom of their pole. He tried to open it, but the clasp was held shut by a combination lock.

By now, many other families had started thinking like Cal. No one else could climb the pole like Emma

Wylot, and no family was able to copy the Rivales' pyramid. People wanted to get inside the chests, and they were trying different four-number combinations. A few were kicking the chests, trying to break them open.

"This is silly, and I have way too much work to do!" Mrs. T. called to Cal. "We're just not a contest kind of family. We'll wait for you in the Flying Monkey."

"Hold on, please!" Cal said. He was reading words carved into the top of the chest. "There's a clue here. It says, 'To open and use the chest, you need to know two things: the birth date of the royalty of marvels . . . and that the time of the message is past!'"

A few contestants around Cal mumbled that they had no idea what that could mean and went back to shaking the poles. But Mrs. T. had stopped in her tracks on the way to the car. "Oh, that first part is easy," she said automatically. "The answer is twelve zero two."

The families close by heard her, and immediately spun the dials. Cal did the same. "She's right!" James shouted, pulling his lock free. "Thanks, Mrs. T.!"

Cal shot her a look. Some people collected snow globes or stamps. His mom hunted strange facts about the ancient Olympics, the speed of a ferret's sneeze, what aardvarks ate—whatever! But this probably wasn't the best time for her to show off her trivia skills.

Mrs. T. shrugged. "*The royalty of marvels* is another way of saying *King Wonder,* and his birthday is December second, or twelve zero two. Doesn't everyone know that?"

If anyone had missed her spilling the answer before, they heard her now. One by one, the rest of the families spun the locks and popped open the chests. Kids and parents laughed, pulling back in surprise as three helium balloons with pictures on them drifted up out of each box. Strings kept them from floating away.

"We like our shoppers to be resourceful and find the best value in our Circles of Dreams!" Mr. Vance yelled. "To help you prove you can be smart shoppers, we put a few other things inside each chest."

Mr. Vance was right. Cal spotted a three-foot-long piece of thin steel and two pieces of wood at the bottom of the chest. What were they supposed to do with these?

Cal held them up for his family to see. They had been walking away. But now they were back at the starting line, like moths drawn to a flame.

His dad had turned his glasses on a slant and was

smiling. "The three balloons tell you what to do with that stuff," he called to Cal. "The balloons are a rebus—it's not too tough!"

Cal looked more closely at the balloons. One had the letter *I*, the second had an eye, and the third had a sheep with a pink bow on its tail. It *was* a rebus!

Cal read the symbols out loud. "I eye sheep." No, he knew in an instant that wasn't right. An eye could mean *see* in a rebus. He tried again. "I see sheep."

"Look at the bow on the sheep's tail," Mr. T. said. "It's a female!"

Right. A female sheep was a ewe. Cal replaced the word *sheep* with *ewe*.

"I see ewe . . . ," Cal said. Then he got it. "I see YOU!"

he yelled, and slapped his hand over his mouth. He was just as bad as the rest of his family at giving away clues.

But it didn't matter if people overheard him. How would a rebus message that said "I see you" help anyone get butterflies off poles? Cal reread the words on the chest, focusing on the second part of the clue: "The time of the message is past!"

The message was "I see you." How would you say that in the past?

"It should be 'I *saw* you,'" he whispered to himself.

"*Saw?*" someone said right next to him. Cal jumped. It was Imo. He knew she couldn't resist cracking the code. She was pulling one earlobe, the way she did when her brain was really humming.

"I've got the answer," she said. "It's a—"

For some reason, her mouth snapped shut. Cal turned to find that Mr. Vance's cameraman was pointing his lens directly at her. Imo went pale, and she put her head down so the spaceship-shaped clip in her hair sparkled in the setting sun, like she was trying to hide.

"What's wrong with you?" Cal asked. "What's the solution?"

Imo didn't answer. Instead, she took the three items from Cal's hands and snapped the pieces of wood on either end of the strip of steel. With her eyes, she made back-and-forth gestures along the pole. Almost as if she were using her gaze to cut the pole. Or *saw* it!

Cal finally understood. "I *saw* you."

Aha! He grabbed one end of the saw that Imo had made, and she held the other. They put the steel blade next to the pole and started pushing and pulling. It took them a second to get the right rhythm as they cut into the pole. Other families had caught on by now and snapped their own saws together. But Imo and Cal had a head start.

They quickly sliced into the wood, and, like a tree, the pole started to fall over.

"Timber!" Mr. Vance cried.

As it tipped over, the top of the Talaskas' pole headed straight for the Wylots. They already had a butterfly, but Cal could see them getting ready to grab this one, too. Leslie Wylot shoved her sister out of the way, trying to get to it first. Her arms reached out to catch it.

Luckily, Cal was a pretty good athlete. He jumped between the falling pole and Leslie. He snagged the stuffed butterfly off the top just before she could touch it, and the pole slammed into the ground. *WHAM!*

"Yes!" Cal said, holding up the silly-looking butterfly

like it was the world's greatest trophy. He turned around so the crowd could see him. A stuffed toy had never felt this good in his fingers.

"And we have our third finalist family!" Mr. Vance shouted. The audience went berserk, yelling and clapping. As Cal jumped up and down, he saw that even his parents were cheering. Bug was spinning in circles with Butler.

Mr. Vance gathered the Talaskas, Wylots, and Rivales together. "Congratulations to the finalists!" he said.

"We're the winners!" Leslie Wylot shouted.

"Not quite," Mr. Vance said with a chuckle. "To make it to the Great Grab Contest, the three families have to survive two more elimination rounds. First, you must create a thirty-second video to show you are perfect Wish Shoppe shoppers! Not only will the winning family keep whatever they grab in King's new store, which will open in a few weeks, but also their video will appear on billboards all over the country!"

Imo got a panicked look on her face. "That's never going to happen," she said under her breath.

Hearing her, Mr. Vance rushed over to Imo. "What's your name, little girl, and where are you from?" he demanded as his cameraman zoomed in.

Little girl? Imo hated being talked down to, and this

should have been enough to send her into a rant. But she just kept her head down. Since when was she so shy?

Finally, Cal stepped in front of her and looked straight into the camera. "We're the Talaskas from Piedmont Place," he said proudly. "And it turns out that we *are* a contest kind of family!"

The next morning at school, Cal met up with James in gym class. They were early and shot a few baskets while they waited for the teacher.

"Stellar performance yesterday, Captain," James said after going in for a layup. He had a habit of wiping his nose with his hand, so Cal gave him an air fist bump.

"Thanks, my man," Cal said. He was still buzzing from the race. "Sorry your family didn't nab a butterfly."

"No big deal," James said. "My dad and I had a blast doing it. Did you convince your parents and Imo to keep going with the contest?"

He glanced across the gym at Imo. Cal and his sister were both in fifth grade because Imo had skipped a grade two years ago. She was at the other basket, shooting with her friend Simone.

"I haven't convinced them yet," Cal said. "But I'm working on it."

Actually, Cal's parents and Imo had come right out and said they had zero interest in the contest. Mrs. T. was way too busy for something so "silly." Mr. T. didn't want to compete against his boss. And they sure as heck didn't want to make a video about their family for the next elimination round.

But Cal was more determined than ever. Just the thought of grabbing whatever he wanted from the Wish Shoppe's aisles of 3-D printers, giant TVs, go-karts, automatic bowling balls—you name it!—was enough to bring a grin to Cal's face. Plus, the whole country would see his family in the Wish Shoppe ads and know how perfect the Talaskas were.

Cal's grin disappeared when Leslie Wylot bounced into the gym, her three perfect braids snapping an angry rhythm. Cal's class had stopped having show-and-tell years ago, but Leslie held her own version pretty much every day. This morning was no different. She carried the Wish Shoppe stuffed butterfly for all to see, as if it were a major movie award. She strutted across the gym and took a seat next to Alison Mangan on the bleachers.

Without missing a beat, Leslie started talking. "I can't wait to get whatever I want in the Great Grab Contest, Alison. I know I get what I wish for every day. But this is different. Because everyone will be watching. I'm so glad we're best friends, Alison. We can tell each other everything!"

The whole gym could hear every loud word she said. People on other planets could hear her. Alison said something, but it was like talking into a hurricane. Cal liked Alison. She laughed at all his jokes, even the dumb ones, and she used to stand up to Leslie. Now Alison did everything Leslie said—and Cal didn't get why.

Leslie just kept rolling along. "It's totally cute and so sad the way those Talaskas think they have a chance to win the contest." She pointed at Imo and then Cal. "Look at them! Aren't they hilarious!"

Cal stopped dribbling. "I'm right in front of you, Leslie."

"Oh, Cal," Leslie said. "Can't you take a joke?"

Before Cal could answer, Ms. Graves rushed into the gym. "Sorry, folks, your gym teacher, Mr. Price, is out sick today. You've just got me."

Cal couldn't have been happier. Ms. Graves was usually their English teacher. Cal was a fan of Ms. Graves. At the beginning of the year, he had almost convinced her he was allergic to homework. *Almost.*

"Why don't we play a game of—" Ms. Graves started to say when the intercom buzzed. The voice of the school secretary came over the speaker. "Ms. Graves? We need your help in the office. Principal Cahill is locked in the supply closet again." A split second later, the intercom buzzed once more. "Better bring Imo Talaska with you."

"I'll be just a minute, Ms. Graves," Imo said, and ran to the locker room to change.

"We have to rescue the principal from his prison of paper clips," Ms. Graves told the class. "I'll return in a few minutes. Until then, behave, and play . . . a gym game . . . or something."

Imo was back in a flash, rushing through the gym to follow Ms. Graves out the door. Imo had put on the overalls she kept at school for helping out with quick fixes. The pockets were filled with tools like screwdrivers, a spud wrench, and even a plugging chisel.

Leslie gave her a once-over. "Nice outfit, Jessie!"

Either Imo didn't hear her or she pretended not to. She just kept moving.

"Knock it off, Leslie," Cal said.

"What? It is *nice*!" But the way Leslie had said *nice* definitely wasn't nice. "I just think it's a shame that my family is going to win the Great Grab Contest and Jessie won't have the chance to grab more things. You know, like those *nice* hair clips from *Star Wars* she always wears."

Cal trotted across the room after his sister. He caught up to her in the hall. "Imo!"

Imo turned around impatiently, tapping her foot. They were standing next to the sports trophy case—a

spot where their mom always stopped when she came to school.

"What is it, Cal?" Imo demanded. Ms. Graves had already turned the corner to the principal's office. A banging sound was coming from the supply closet.

"Why don't you stand up to her?" Cal asked.

"Who? Leslie?" Imo said. "Who cares what she says? And Jessie *is* my real name."

It was true. Imo's real name was Jessie. But her nickname, Imo, was so much better. Her first word as a baby hadn't been *Mommy* or something like *apple*—she'd said "in my opinion." After her toy elephant had splashed into a bowl of milk, she'd fished it out, licked it, and said, "In my opinion . . . blech!"

As she got older, she kept it up. During dinner when Mrs. T. had forgotten to thaw the fish sticks, she said, "Fish sticks make good Popsicles, in my opinion." Another time, she said, "In my opinion, ghost stories are better without ghosts." Just a month ago: "To keep the water in the kitchen sink at forty psi, in my opinion, we'll need to exercise that valve with sliding-head pliers."

In my opinion this. *In my opinion* that.

The Talaskas started calling her IMO for short, and it stuck.

"Just let Leslie play her games," Imo said. "Stuff she says doesn't matter."

"But it does," Cal insisted. "It matters how people treat us. That's why this Great Grab Contest—"

"Ugh with the contest!" Imo said. "I told you I don't want to be in front of cameras anymore." Down the hall, the banging was getting louder. "Look, I've got to go." She took off.

When Cal went back into the gym, Leslie had pulled out the red rubber balls. "We're playing dodgeball," she announced to the twenty-two kids.

A few of them gasped, and one boy shouted, "Dodge-ball was outlawed after you lost your temper last time!"

"Besides, it's totally dangerous!" Sheila Hanahan screeched. She was the smallest girl in the class.

Leslie rolled her eyes. "Oh please. Dangerous? That idea is just a conspiracy by badminton companies. And I know about big companies. After all, my dad runs the biggest one in the state. . . . What? It's not bragging if you can Google it."

Cal didn't want anyone getting smacked by a rubber

ball. He trotted over to the canister of lightweight foam balls. Imo had made them for kids who couldn't catch. She had sprayed them with a static glue so they stuck to hands instead of bouncing away.

"We'll use the balls Imo made," Cal said.

Leslie sighed impatiently. "Fine, fine, whatever."

They started to break up into teams. Leslie was one captain and Cal the other. Kids drifted toward Cal.

"I have a fun way of making teams," Leslie announced. "Whoever wants my family to win the Wish Shoppe Great Grab Contest, come on over to my side."

The other kids looked at each other, confused, and still headed for Cal.

"Let me put it another way," Leslie said. "Whoever's parents work for my father in some shape or form, I'm sure you'll make the right decision."

Leslie often made hints that her dad could fire anyone. Most of the kids shrugged, grabbed a ball from the canister, and walked over to Leslie's side. Only James stayed put next to Cal. The two were going to get slaughtered. Buried under an avalanche of yellow balls.

"Poor Cal," Leslie said with a fake smile. "It's not personal. People just have to know their place in life, that's all. There are the winners and there are the losers." She cocked her arm with the ball and waited for everyone else to do the same. "Are you ready, Cal?" Leslie asked.

"Hold on," Cal said. He needed to stall for time. "My shoe's untied."

"Make it fast," Leslie said.

While he crouched with his head down, pretending to tie his shoe, Cal spoke quickly to the class. "Look, I know you all think you've made a decision. But I want you to look at that ball in your hands. If you had to really choose in a split second, where would you throw it?" He took a breath. "Listen to your heart, not your fear."

When Cal stood back up, all the balls were still aimed directly at him. And Leslie was grinning at him. "Sounds good, Cal," she said. "When will you learn? My family and I always get what we want. Here we go!"

At that moment, the gym door slammed open and the noise startled everyone. Ms. Graves and Imo were back. The sound of the door was like a starter cannon, and the kids threw the balls without thinking. *Phlit! Phlit!* Balls whizzed through the air, finding their target.

"Holy Aristotle," Cal said under his breath. The kids had listened to their hearts—and Cal—after all.

Leslie was covered in the static balls from her sparkly sneakers to her braids. She looked like the cartoon character called Princess Fuzzy in cotton ball ads on TV. Except Leslie was bright yellow.

Cal knew the power of nicknames. He had seen Leslie use them to put other kids down or just for fun. He knew that if he opened his mouth and said, "Hey, Princess Fuzzy!" the nickname would stick to her for months, or even years.

But he didn't say it. Instead, he tossed his ball aside and walked over to pull the foam balls off Leslie. Ms. Graves and Imo hurried over, too. But Leslie wanted none of it. Red-faced, she pushed them away and rushed toward the locker room in a huff.

"My family always gets what

we want!" she yelled over her shoulder, her words muffled by the yellow ball stuck on her collar. "Alison, come with me. Now!"

Alison shrugged and followed her. Watching them go, Ms. Graves looked confused. "All right, everyone," she said to the rest of the class. "Give me fifty . . ." Ms. Graves paused. "What's a gym thing? Right. Fifty jumping jacks, please."

As they bounced up and down, James shook his head. "You shouldn't have done that, Cal."

Cal knew James was right. He shouldn't have let Leslie get to him. Cal blamed the excitement of the Great Grab Contest for pushing him a little too far. He shrugged, trying to act like it was no big deal. "She can't get her dad to fire everyone in Hawkins."

"Maybe not everyone," James agreed. "But how about just one person?"

"**H**i, Cal?" said Sarah, the babysitter, when Cal walked around to his backyard after school. "Someone left a message for your parents? On the answering machine? Mr. Wylot, I think?"

Uh-oh, Cal thought. Had Leslie already told her dad about gym class? Was Mr. T.'s job at the Wylots' factory in trouble?

Sarah was upside down, her legs hooked around the highest bar on the swing set. The college student's curly hair was so long, it dragged back and forth in the grass. Bug and Butler were sitting nearby on the ground, staring at her, both their heads tilted slightly to the left.

On days when Mrs. T. was busy taking sports stars around Hawkins to give their speeches, she hired Sarah to watch Bug. Everything Sarah said sounded like a question. Maybe that was why she could get Bug to chill out, although no one else could. He and Butler could stare at her for days. And when they weren't staring, they were trying to impress her with their "world-famous" B&B Scooter Madness Stunt.

The fake stunt always went the same way. Bug started by scratching Butler behind the ears and grabbing on to a rope tied to his collar. Butler would race ahead, pulling Bug on his scooter toward a seat cushion on the patio. At the last second, just as they were about to crash, they'd make a wide turn and avoid the cushion.

Bug's hands would shoot up in the air like he was a champion who had just accomplished a dangerous feat. He'd say some kind of gibberish while Butler let out his trademark bark—"Rabbo!"—with his tail twirling.

Cal shook his head to clear it. He had much more important things to worry about. "Is my dad home yet?" he asked. "Has he heard the message?"

"He's home?" Sarah said. "But he went straight to the kitchen? He asked if I could stay for a few more minutes while he works on his music?"

Good. Until Cal could figure out what to do, he had to find a way to keep his dad from playing that message.

He didn't know if Mr. Wylot would really fire his dad because Leslie demanded it. But even if Mr. Wylot was just upset, the message could ruin Cal's hopes of entering the Great Grab Contest. It would be one more reason his parents might give for not making the video.

Cal could hear Imo working on the other side of the overgrown bush on the patio. And suddenly he knew how to distract his parents so they wouldn't hear the message, at least for a while.

"Thanks, Sarah!" Cal said. "Hang in there!"

Imo had changed into her overalls again. She was eating an apple while working on one of her nutty projects. Imo had built a platform twice as tall as Cal. It had a ramp down the front, and on top sat a long board with six wheels. Whatever the wheeled thing was, it could be just what Cal needed to cause a ruckus.

"Wow, Imo," Cal said. "You've gone to a whole new

level with this . . . go-kart . . . sled . . . best Imo creation ever."

Imo rolled her eyes and took another bite from her apple. "It's a lawn luge. Before I make spaceships, I might as well start on the ground." She finished turning a bolt on the ramp with her wrench. "And, no, you can't ride it."

Sometimes Cal had to fine-tune his sweet talk. "We don't do enough as brother and sister," he said, putting a hand over his heart. "We can ride it together, Imo."

"Ugh, weird, Cal," Imo said. She tapped one of the back wheels with her wrench. "Besides, this wheel isn't working quite right . . . and I don't know why."

Then, as Imo tugged her earlobe, Cal could see his sister's brain start to sizzle. When she set her sights on a problem, she *had* to solve it.

"Hold on!" he said before he completely lost her.

Too late. "Here, take this," she said, and handed Cal

the half-eaten apple. Mumbling formulas about energy and wheels, she wandered off toward her fort in the corner of the backyard. Designed to look like a sheriff's office from the Old West, the one-room fort had been Cal's eleventh-birthday present a few months ago. Imo had taken it over and turned it into her workshop, where she dreamed up inventions.

When Imo was inside the fort, Cal asked softly, "So I can ride the luge after all, Imo? If your answer is yes, don't say anything."

He gave it a second. Nothing. Putting the apple in his jacket pocket, he scrambled up the ramp. From up there on the wobbly platform, Cal could see past their backyard fence into the Rivales' yard.

Cal lay on his back on the lawn luge and put his hands to the sides to push off. *Crack!* One of the back wheels snapped free and tumbled off the platform.

"Uh, Imo, quick question!" Cal yelled. He was teetering on the edge of the ramp. "Would your luge work without one of the wheels?"

"Sure," Imo called from her workshop. "But only if you want to spin out of control and crash into the patio!"

"Wait, what?"

Before he could stop it, the luge shot down the ramp, dragging to one side, where the wheel should have been. He nearly plunged over the edge, and then slammed onto the patio.

Umph! The luge spun completely around. Now it was flying across the concrete toward the house.

Cal zipped on the luge through the open back door and shot into the kitchen. His dad was at the table with his back to Cal, his fingers pounding on the wood surface.

"Dad!" Cal shouted.

But it was no good. Mr. T. wore sound-blocking headphones that helped him concentrate. They also made him look like a giant-eared alien as he loudly sang, *"Rutherford B. Hayes, why oh why do you hate mayonnaise?"*

Mr. T. loved to make up songs. He said it was relaxing, especially after a long day at his accounting job. The family didn't have a piano, so Mr. T. pretended the kitchen table was a keyboard.

"Dad, a little help here!" Cal called out.

Mr. T. just kept crooning about sandwich spread as Cal knocked against a chair and zoomed out of the kitchen. With a jolt, the front wheels hit the living room carpet. The luge stopped dead on the shag . . . but Cal kept moving.

Ziipp!

He shot off the luge and into the room like pizza sliding off a tray. He crashed into the files Mrs. T. kept stacked along the wall. Notebook pages and sticky notes flew up and whirled around him like confetti as he tumbled into the corner.

Finally, Cal came to a halt on his side, and he stayed there for a second. Was he in one piece? Yes, thanks to the cushion of his mom's paperwork.

After a few seconds, Cal saw that his plan had gone horribly wrong—or horribly right. Talk about a distraction! The living room was a disaster. He stumbled to his feet and—

Wham!

Cal was tackled from the side by something huge and furry. Papers went flying again as he went down. And then a wet nose was snuffling at his pockets.

What the heck was Butler doing?

Oh, right, Cal remembered. The half-eaten apple! This was Imo's fault!

He tried to stand up. Butler knocked him over again,

this time getting the apple out of his jacket. Reaching for balance, Cal tipped over a side table. The answering machine on the table clattered to the floor with a *BEEP!*

His parents, Imo, Bug, and Sarah rushed into the living room. Mrs. T.'s eyes went wide as she took in all the destruction. "What the Gouda is going on?" she asked.

"The Butler did it!" Cal said. This time, it was true. Well, kind of.

"Thanks for test-driving the luge for me, Cal," Imo said, and then she burst out laughing. She held up a screw. She must have removed it from the lawn luge's wheel while Cal had been talking to her.

Imo had set him up. Cal should've known!

Butler chomped happily on the apple and rolled over . . . right onto the answering machine. It beeped again and announced, "Playing first new message."

No!

Instead of distracting all of them so they wouldn't play the message, Cal had actually gathered an audience.

"Hello, Talaskas," a voice said over the machine. It wasn't Mr. Wylot. It was *Mrs.* Wylot.

Cal didn't know what to do. He was tempted to dance

or just start yelling to keep them from listening. But his parents would hear the message sooner or later.

"I apologize for not sending out our usual high-quality invitations!" Mrs. Wylot was saying in her frantic voice. Every time Cal heard her speak, she sounded as if she were on board a sinking ship. "We'd love to have you over to our estate for a pool party and a big surprise, three Sundays from now at four PM, if you're free—"

"Of course they're free," they could hear Mr. Wylot say in the background. "What else do they have to do? Just hang up."

Click. The line went dead.

Cal didn't feel the relief he'd thought he would. This seemed just like something Leslie would plan as revenge for gym class. In fact, all the Talaskas were staring at the machine in confusion. For the moment, the chaos Cal had caused was forgotten.

"A party?" Mr. T. asked. "The Wylots want to invite *us* to a party?"

"What do they mean by *surprise*?" Imo asked. She glanced around as if the surprise might jump up out of nowhere.

"Oh, I don't know," Mrs. T. said. "Maybe they just want to be nice? Don't you think, Sarah?"

"Yes?" Sarah replied. As always, she answered with a question. And Cal thought that made a lot of sense, especially because he had his own big question:

What were the Wylots up to?

"**W**hat's the big surprise?" James asked. It was the same thing Cal had been asking himself since hearing the message yesterday.

Cal and James were leaning against the Talaskas' backyard fence, watching the Rivales next door like they were a reality TV show.

The Rivales didn't mind the attention. Not only were they finalists in the Great Grab Contest, they were professional coupon clippers, tae kwon do masters, and champion synchronized swimmers. They were used to people watching them.

Right now, they were heading into the huge tent they had set up in the backyard. The parents and the triplets moved in exactly the same way. They reminded Cal of the workings of a clock. Maybe a cuckoo clock.

James raised a hand. "Hello, Rivales!"

The Rivales didn't stop, but each of their five heads turned as if they were prairie dogs. With their slicked-back hair and black clothes, it was hard to tell which family member was which. Without smiling, the Rivales silently waved back in perfect unison.

Cal laughed as if they had just performed an amazing trick. "Holy Aristotle! That's amazing!" he cheered. But instead of taking a bow or laughing along, the Rivales nodded and disappeared into the tent.

Cal and James shared a quick look that said, *Can you believe it?*

And then Cal got back to James's question. "I don't know what the Wylots' big surprise is."

Cal was worried about what Leslie might have planned. But the party was weeks away, and he had more pressing problems.

"If I'm going to win the Great Grab Contest, I have to get my family to make a video," Cal said. "Just think how it will be when I win and grab the Wonder World Video Game System!"

James's face got serious. *"Add more wonder to your world and play* inside *the game!"* he said, sounding just like a TV announcer. James could copy anyone's voice. Once he'd pretended to be the school secretary on the phone and asked Principal Cahill to go buy a tin of anchovies.

Wonder World had been invented by King Wonder himself, and it was sold only at Wish Shoppes. It cost as much as a car, but for good reason. It was the only game that turned a player's real life into a game. Players plugged in the game, and no matter where they were, the game adapted. In other words, players could control the world around them. It was the perfect game for Cal!

"We could be playing Wonder World in my basement right now!" Cal glanced back at his house. The drooping gutters. The peeling paint. The trees that seemed so exhausted they could barely keep themselves from collapsing onto the roof. He loved his giant, rambling house and how it looked like a ship that had run aground—but he wasn't sure everyone else did.

"The video just has to show that my family is the perfect family to shop at Wish Shoppe," Cal said, "and I'll win."

James always looked away when Cal said the words *perfect family*. Cal knew what he was thinking. The Talaskas weren't as rich as the Wylots. And they didn't move as smoothly as the Rivales. But who cared? Cal knew if people could just see how great his family was, the Talaskas would easily win.

"I can help you with the video entry," James said.

"Thanks, my man," Cal said, clapping his shoulder. "But I actually think it's better if I try it alone. I know my family. They won't be able to resist my special plan."

"Are you going with Strategic Pestering?" James asked.

"No," Cal said. "I need something a little fancier."

A whole day of "Take me to the fair, please," repeated

over and over, had worked when he was seven years old. But he was much more skilled now. "I'm going with Turbo Adorable," Cal said.

A car pulled into the Talaskas' driveway. It was James's older sister, and she beeped the horn.

"Got to go," James said. "Good luck, Captain."

Cal waved to James's sister as his friend got in the car. She waved back cautiously. Cal knew she was thinking about the time he convinced her to make—and eat—a pint of tuna-fish ice cream.

Everything was ready for Cal to put his plan into action. He started by propping his old, beat-up camera, which took video, on the patio table. Then he shouted through the screen door into the house, "Mom! Do you have a second?"

His mom came out of the living room, her pencil still in her hand. "What is it, honey?"

"If you put all the products at a Wish Shoppe in a line, how many times would it go around the planet?" he asked.

"Hmm," Mrs. T. said, tapping the pencil against her leg. "I'd have to figure that out. Why are you asking?"

"No reason," Cal said sweetly. "I just know you're the best at trivia, and I'm trying to think like you."

"Um, okay," Mrs. T. said.

She stayed for a second, and Cal was glad. He wanted her to see how he was imitating her. Also, he wanted his whole family to think he was struggling to make the video without them. He hoped they would feel bad and decide to take part after all.

Pushing his hair back the way his mom did, he faced the camera and said, "I want a home gym."

"Cal . . . ," his mom said from inside. Was she already about to crack?

But then Mrs. T.'s desk phone rang, and she had to go answer it. Cal moved on to the next person on his list.

"Imo!" he shouted in the direction of her workshop.

"What?" she called without opening the door.

"Is this something you'd wear?" he asked.

She peeked her head out and saw him holding up a yellow T-shirt with a flower on it.

"Oh brother," she said, and closed the door again.

Cal hoped she was still watching through a crack. He put on the T-shirt and looked at the camera. Getting as close to Imo's voice as he could, he said, "I'd like a spacecraft laboratory."

He knew he looked adorable.

A minute later, Cal called, "Dad!" and slid on a giant

pair of fake glasses. After singing a short song about tinfoil in his dad's voice, he yelled for Bug. Cal lifted his hands in the air like a champion, marched around, and barked, "Rabbo!"

When Cal started to put on one of Butler's old dog collars, his parents and Imo finally came out onto the patio.

"Okay, this is just—" Imo said.

"The cutest thing ever?" Cal finished for her.

She shook her head. "No, really, really creepy. Stop dressing up and acting like us."

"But—"

"If you do," Mr. T. said, "we'll make the video with you, okay? But only the video. And then that's the end of all this contest business."

"Your dad and I both work very hard during the day," Mrs. T. said. "So we don't have time for nonsense."

"Thanks!" Cal said. "And, Dad, I'm sure Mr. Wylot would want you to do it." At the name Mr. Wylot, his dad's face clouded over. Cal needed to change the subject quickly. "The deadline to submit the video is seven o'clock tomorrow."

Imo said, "That's just twenty-five hours away."

Bug barked to Butler. The meaning was clear. It was impossible.

"No, Bug," Cal said. "That's plenty of time. Imo, you build the sets. Mom, we need more facts about the store. Dad can write the jingle—you know, catchy music that will get stuck in people's heads."

Mrs. T. frowned. "Let's leave Dad out of this. Mr. Wylot is being a major—" She interrupted herself and started again. "Work is very challenging for your dad right now."

"No, Mom, we can't leave anyone out," Cal said. "We have to be the *perfect* family. Dad is always picking words out of the dictionary—like, I don't know . . ."

Imo chimed in, *"Polyphagous?"*

"Exactly," Cal said. "So writing a jingle about Wish Shoppe should be a breeze!"

Mr. T. nodded. "I'll come up with something on my lunch break. What about you, Cal? What are you going to do?"

"I'll write the script and direct, of course."

Bug barked again. He wanted a job, too.

Cal shook his head. "Bug, you'll just be Bug."

By the next afternoon, the Talaskas' backyard was transformed. Imo had used old cardboard from refrigerator boxes to build a set where they could shoot the video. She had turned the cardboard into walls and started to paint them white with blue trim, just like the walls in Wish Shoppe.

It looked amazing. Then Bug dipped Butler's tail in blue paint and chased the dog around the backyard. Butler's tail smeared blue paint all over the patio and one of the cardboard walls, so Imo ended up painting the whole set blue.

When Mr. T. got home from work, his gaze landed on the muddy ditch Cal had dug. It was his version of the River of Low Prices, which ran between the Wish Shoppe and the parking lot.

Cal wondered if an insect was crawling on his dad's face. Mr. T.'s cheek was twitching, and a vein in his neck had popped out. He turned around and went inside. Cal could hear him counting to ten. When Mr. T. came back out with Mrs. T., he didn't look quite as red.

"All right, I'm ready, Mr. Director," he said, turning his glasses on a slant. "How can we make this thing soar?"

Mrs. T. smiled, and Cal handed his dad a script. Mr. T. flipped through it, and his eyes widened with each page. "Uh . . . okay. Whatever you say."

Ten minutes later, the family had taken their positions.

Cal put the camera back on the patio table. He pressed RECORD and rushed to his place.

"Action!" Cal called out.

Imo had glued a handle on the lawn luge so it looked like a huge shopping cart. Mr. T. pushed it in front of the camera.

"Hello . . . Talaska . . . family!" Mr. T. said in a wooden voice, reading from the script.

"Why, hello there, uh, stranger!" Mrs. T. said back, reading her line. "How are you?"

"I am . . . super great," Mr. T. said. "You know why? Because I am shopping at Wish Shoppe, where I can get whatever I want!" He pretended to pull a mask off his face. "And guess what! It's me, your Talaska dad!"

"Oh! What a, uh, surprise!" Mrs. T. said in fake

shock. "We were having so much fun shopping here at Wish Shoppe that we didn't even know it was you!"

Cal jumped out in front of the camera. "We're the Talaskas!"

Imo threw a bucket of water toward the set just as Butler bumped into her. The water missed its target and splashed onto Cal's pants.

Gasping, Cal stopped acting. "Why did you do that?" he demanded.

"It's rain!" Imo said.

Cal's script said there should be a rain shower, a snowstorm, and a mild hurricane. He wanted to show that the Talaskas were the perfect Wish Shoppe family under any conditions.

"You ready for the snow?" Imo asked.

"No!" Cal shouted.

"What about the butterflies?"

Cal shook his head. "Let's just say our lines and talk about what we want at Wish Shoppe. You go first, Imo."

Imo faced the camera, and she suddenly looked as terrified as if a stampede of buffalo were about to flatten her. Cal didn't get it. How could she argue to the death with him about the perfect temperature of milk but then get frozen by a tiny camera?

Cal stood behind Imo and said in her voice, "My name is Imo. I want a spacecraft laboratory. My mom wants a gym. My dad will grab an orchestra. My handsome, so-much-smarter-than-me older brother will take a video game system. My little brother and our dog want something amazing, too, but only they know what it is!"

That was their cue to start singing the jingle that Mr. T. had written. The family stood together by the muddy moat and sang:

"Oh, Wish Shoppe, you cause our hearts to hop!
Please never stop making those high prices drop!
Oh, Wish Shoppe, you give the best impression!
We have just one or two quick questions:
In your name, what's with the extra P?
Isn't it time to maybe set it free?
Into the River of Low Prices let it flow—"

"Hee," Mrs. T. said in a burst of laughter while the others kept singing:

"It's something we need to know—"

"Hee hee," Imo said.

The hee-hees were like a virus, leaping from one

person to the next. Cal could feel his shoulders shake. *NO! Control. This is too important.*

Still looking into the camera, he tried to keep a straight face. He could feel his mom and Imo struggling, too. Finally, it popped out of Cal's mouth. "Hee hee."

His dad joined in. "Hee. Hee. Hee. Hee." And then his mom. Soon the only ones singing were Butler, who was howling, and Bug, who chirped nonsense sounds. The others were gasping for breath as their laughter picked up steam.

"What's . . . with the . . . extra *P*!" Mrs. T. managed to say, tears streaming down her face as she clutched her sides.

"Let it *flow*!" Mr. T. added, and doubled over. "Set it *free*!"

"What rhymes with *free*, Dad?" Imo asked, collapsing on the ground. "It starts with a *P*!"

Cal stumbled around, unable to stop laughing, and then fell over next to Imo. Soon the Talaskas were rolling on the grass like hysterical hyenas. With his own high-pitched giggles, Bug dove onto the heap. And then Butler jumped on top of all of them. The dog flipped over and started squirming on his back, rubbing against the family and somehow making everything seem funnier.

Cal was laughing so hard, he was worried he would actually set free his own extra P.

"Cal!" Mrs. T. wheezed. "Your pants!"

Oh no, Cal thought, realizing what he must look like. His pants were soaked from the fake rain!

"The Butler did it!" he managed to gasp. His words brought even more waves of laughter, and everyone clutched their stomachs. Finally, after thirty more seconds of complete nuttiness, Cal staggered to his feet and looked at his watch. Oh man. They only had an hour to finish the video and upload it to the Wish Shoppe site.

"All right! All right!" he said, wiping the tears from his face and spitting out a clump of Butler's fur. "From the top!"

They ran through Cal's script quickly. This time, they managed to do it without anyone bursting into hysterics.

"That's a wrap, people," Cal said. "Imo, can you fix it up and add the music and sound effects?"

"Sure," Imo said, taking the camera to make the changes on it.

Half an hour later, when she announced she was done, Cal glanced at his watch.

"Good timing," he said. "Ten minutes to go until the video is due."

Imo perched in front of the computer and opened the Wish Shoppe website. "Uh-oh," she said.

"What is it?" Cal asked. "What's wrong?"

"With our dial-up connection," Imo said, "it will take over fifteen minutes to upload the video."

"We're not going to make it," Mrs. T. said. "There's not enough time."

Cal put his head in his hands. "No, no, no," he groaned.

Tugging her ear, Imo announced, "Then it's a good

thing I can optimize the connection and have it uploaded in nine minutes."

"Do it!" Cal shouted, and Imo got to work. She plugged the camera into the computer, and her fingers flew across the keyboard.

"Go, go, go!" the whole family was chanting. They watched the bar that showed how much of the upload was left. It was going to be close. Then—*bing!*

"We did it!" Cal said.

Just barely. Seconds later, the contest screen was replaced by these words:

Hello, dreamers! The time for Great Grab Contest entries has passed. Good luck to our three finalists. The two winning families of the next round will be revealed in three weeks on the Wish Shoppe billboard in Hawkins, Michigan! Till then, wish well!

—King Wonder

"What do we do now?" Cal asked.

Mrs. T. answered with the hardest words for Cal to hear.

"We wait."

To Cal, waiting was like bathing in his brother's used bathwater. It was torture.

Every day, Cal rode his bike by the Wish Shoppe billboard on Palmer's Farm. He would stare at the sign for almost an hour, hoping King Wonder would announce the two finalist families early.

Instead, the electronic sign showed the same commercial over and over: King Wonder running around a Wish Shoppe with his Butterfly of Savings. The butterfly was a direct descendant of the one that King had had as a kid, and it lived for a month in each new store he built. In the ad, King flapped his arms like a butterfly. He glided around the Wish Shoppe's confusing

Nine Circles of Dreams, or departments, like it was the easiest thing in the world.

Cal thought he'd go crazy from the waiting. The days seemed to stretch on forever. The rest of the family didn't have the same problem.

Bug and Butler practiced their fake B&B Scooter Madness Stunt in the backyard. Bug scratched behind Butler's ears and grabbed on to a rope on his collar. Butler took off, pulling Bug on his scooter toward the patio seat cushion. At the last second, they made a wide turn to miss it. They did this again and again.

Mrs. T. was keeping busy with her work. She brought a famous pole-vaulter to town. He spoke at Wylot Auditorium about leaping over obstacles in life. Cal went to listen to the speech. It had mushy parts and funny lines, but nothing about waiting. So it wasn't overly helpful.

Then it was the day when the last two finalist families would be announced. Well, kind of. It was 12:01 AM, and Cal was lying in bed wide awake. His mind was racing. Whose videos would be picked—the Rivales', the Wylots', or the Talaskas'?

Bug's bed was across the room, and Cal could hear him mumbling something in his sleep. Snuggled up next to Bug, a sleeping Butler grunted, "Rabbo," as if he agreed with whatever Bug was saying.

Cal tried everything to get back to sleep. At 4:30 AM, he finally gave up.

★　★　★

He was in the kitchen waiting for his family when they got up hours later. Bug came bounding down in his stunt-car driver outfit, complete with bright-purple helmet and neon-green goggles.

Why was Bug wearing his favorite clothes? Cal wondered. Then it hit him.

Oh man. The Wylots' party. The contest had pushed it out of his head. For some reason, he'd never noticed that the Great Grab announcement was on the same day as the party.

Mr. T. was right behind Bug. "Sorry, little man," Mr. T. said to him. "Today's a big party. You've got to change into other clothes."

Under the helmet, Bug's face started to scrunch.

"BTA!" Imo said, coming down the stairs. She was wearing her overalls, her tool belt, and at least eight hair clips shaped like spaceships from *Star Wars*.

Mr. T. looked at Bug to see if a tantrum might be on

its way. He didn't seem to like what he saw. "Okay, okay," Mr. T. said. "I guess we'll all wear whatever we want."

Bug liked that idea. His face unscrunched and he barked.

"We can't go to the party," Cal said. "We have to be at the billboard for the big announcement."

His mom had just come into the kitchen, still in her robe. "We'll go to the party first," Mrs. T. said. "And then we'll drive by the billboard to check out who won."

"Sounds like a plan," Mr. T. said, and yawned.

Cal could tell that no one in his family thought they had a shot in today's elimination round. But he also knew better than to argue with his parents this early in the morning. It would only backfire.

Instead, he turned his sights on Imo and her overalls. "You know Leslie is just going to make fun of you, right?" he said.

"Why?" Imo said, touching her spaceship hair clips. "Because the *Millennium Falcon* doesn't match my eyes?"

But he could tell she knew what he meant. Cal decided to let it drop.

★ ★ ★

When the Talaskas arrived at the Wylots' mansion, they went straight to the backyard, which was the size of a football field. The entire town had been invited. Hundreds of people were chatting in small groups around the party, but everyone looked a little nervous. Cal knew they were all thinking the same thing: What was the big surprise?

A line of waiters in tuxedos held trays of glasses filled with ice-cold water. Toward the back fence were six barbecue pits with sizzling chicken, steaks, and potatoes. The smells were amazing. Drool dripped from Cal's lips before he could catch it.

But the barbecue pits were blocked off from the crowd by thick velvet ropes. Guests who got too close were hit by little spitballs that shot from the trees behind the pits. *Splat!* Ms. Graves was struck between the eyes. *Splot!* The mailman got hit right on the nose.

After that, everyone kept their distance. Cal wandered off, looking for unguarded snacks and to see if James was there yet. As he walked, he saw a life-sized, gold-covered statue of Mr. Wylot. And beyond it was a pool that held more water than Lake Michigan.

The five Rivales were the only ones swimming in the pool. Well, kind of swimming. Mr. and Mrs. Rivale and the triplets were performing a pretty wacky routine, moving through the water like synchronized otters.

"What are they *doing* in there?" Leslie Wylot said. Cal turned. Leslie and Alison Mangan were walking past him toward the pool. Cal was glad Leslie was too busy focusing on other people to bother Imo.

He shrugged. "It is a pool party, right? The Rivales are just going for a swim."

"Well, I guess there *is* plenty of room in the pool," Leslie said, stroking her braids. "After all, it's the largest one in the county. That's not bragging, you know, because you can Google it."

Cal rolled his eyes. Alison smiled and rolled her eyes, too. Leslie saw it.

"Fetch me a glass of water, would you, best friend?" Leslie said to Alison. Alison's smile disappeared.

"Sure, Leslie, no problem," Alison said in an embarrassed whisper.

"She does whatever I say," Leslie said proudly after Alison left. "My family's company is growing all over the world. Her dad might—or might not—get a promotion from my father. Keeps her on her toes."

"So not cool," Cal said.

"Ground Control to Leslie," Imo said. She had come up behind them. "We regret to inform you that you seem to have lost contact with reality."

"Oh, you Talaskas," Leslie said, as if disappointed. "You still can't take a joke. But I think that's about to change."

Before Cal could respond, a loud screech filled the air, and everyone turned. Mr. Wylot stood on the back deck, tapping a microphone. Cal and Imo joined their family as the rest of the party drifted toward Mr. Wylot. Leslie walked like a princess up the steps and posed proudly next to her dad. Her mom and her older sister, Emma, were already there.

"Welcome to my estate!" Mr. Wylot boomed into the microphone. Several people covered their ears, but Mr. Wylot didn't seem to notice.

"You might be wondering why we haven't served any food yet," he said, wiping crumbs off his chin. "I like the people around me to be hungry. Especially the people who work for me. And, let's face it . . . that's just about everyone here."

"Ha! Ha!" Alison's dad laughed, but no one else did.

Mr. Wylot gave him an annoyed look, then continued. "I want to introduce you to our daughters, Leslie and Emma. Watch out for Emma's little booby traps around the estate—she's quite a military genius, that one. My wife, Olga, and I are so proud of the good work our girls do in the community."

Leslie and Emma took a bow. Emma was holding an

extra-long blow tube. Cal realized she had been firing the spitballs.

"In fact, it was my darling Leslie who helped me come up with today's big surprise," Mr. Wylot said.

Uh-oh, Cal thought. Leslie was grinning straight at Cal, and she mouthed the words *Ready for another joke?*

"And here to introduce the surprise is . . ." Mr. Wylot paused and then shouted, "Mr. Paddy Vance, Vice President of Fun at Wish Shoppe!"

Mr. Vance bounced up onto the deck. Mr. Wylot stepped aside so he could use the microphone.

"Hello, ladies and gents!" Mr. Vance cried, waving both hands at the crowd. "First I want to thank Mr. Wylot for having us here and for convincing Wish Shoppe founder King Wonder to have this elimination round in such a comfortable setting!"

Cal couldn't believe it. They were going to eliminate one of the families now?

"What about the billboard?" he shouted. Mr. T. touched his shoulder. "Sorry," Cal said more quietly. "What about the billboard, sir? I thought you were going to reveal the winners on Palmer's Farm."

Mr. Vance gave him a wink. "Mr. Palmer decided

he didn't want the crowds to come back. And then Mr. Wylot made a generous donation to the, uh . . . Wish Shoppe . . . charity. . . ."

"In other words," the fire chief, Mr. Carmody, grumbled, "Mr. Wylot paid money and got his way."

Pretending not to hear, Mr. Vance kept grinning. "Here's what's going to happen today. Three finalist families made videos about being the world's best Wish Shoppe shoppers: the Wylots, the Rivales, and the Tal-Tal . . . ?"

"Talaskas!" Cal said.

"And the Talaskas," Mr. Vance said. "We're going to show the videos they sent in . . . right now!"

A large screen rose out of the deck behind him. "That's the largest home video screen in North America," Leslie said loudly to Mr. Vance. "Again, not bragging. Google it."

Mr. Vance nodded eagerly as if he would do just that. Then he announced, "The two families that get the loudest applause on the Audience Love Meter will move on to the final round of the Great Grab Contest. So get ready to clap your hearts out!"

A second, much smaller screen slid up next to the

first. This one had the words AUDIENCE LOVE METER over a dial that looked like a car's speedometer.

"King Wonder, owner of Wish Shoppe, is proud to announce the three finalist families in the Great Grab Contest!" Mr. Vance said. "The first video is from the Wylot family!"

A deep voice blasted out of the speakers on the deck. "In a world filled with simple, average people, only one family can dominate and lead. Only one name can rise above all others. And that name is . . . WYLOT!"

The screen filled with an image of the Wylots sprinting like action heroes down a store aisle. Emma pushed a shopping cart with Leslie crouched inside. All four wore full-length fur coats and had bandanas over their faces like bank robbers from the Old West.

Leslie pointed, and lightning bolts shot out of her finger, knocking a giant cotton candy machine off a shelf and into their cart. Mr. Wylot raised both hands and lifted a washing machine into the cart—as if with his mind. Emma performed wild karate moves and chopped a mini refrigerator in half. Mrs. Wylot spun around and became a tornado that sucked in items from the shelves. Lamps, dog beds, stoves, an iguana—all magically flew through the air and into their cart.

Cal's stomach sank. His family couldn't compete with this. It was like watching a Hollywood blockbuster.

The video finished with a huge explosion. *BLAM!* The crowd gasped, and Cal thought he felt his hair blow back.

Mr. Vance grabbed the microphone. "So, folks, what'd you think of the Wylots' video?" he cried. "Remember, your applause will determine the winner!"

A few people in the audience clapped, and the Audience Love Meter ticked up to 16 percent.

"They can scare us into coming to the party," an old man muttered, "but they can't make us clap."

As if to prove him wrong, Mr. Wylot made a twirling signal with his hand. The waiters dropped their trays onto the grass, and they burst into cheers noisy enough to make cheerleaders cover their ears.

The arrow on the meter ticked up to 65 percent. Mr. Mangan clapped and hooted even more loudly, and the Audience Love Meter rose to 72 percent.

"Not a bad score!" Mr. Vance said. "Next up, we have the video from the Rivale family!"

Cal looked for the Rivales. They were right next to him, dripping wet in their swimsuits and standing perfectly still.

"Good luck," Cal said, and they nodded at him in unison.

The Rivales' video popped up on the screen. It showed a single can of corn in a spotlight in a dark tent.

So that's what the Rivales have been up to inside their backyard tent! Cal thought.

With their slicked-back dark hair and black unitards, the Rivales surrounded the can of corn and just stared at it. Slowly . . . very slowly . . . they each moved one hand in little circles around the can at exactly the same time.

Then the screen went black except for the single word *FIN*.

The video ended.

People were stunned. Mr. Vance snapped himself out of some kind of trance and finally said, "Let's hear applause for the Rivales!"

There was nothing. Not even from the Rivales. Finally, Cal gave a little clap. That started a small ripple, and the arrow on the Audience Love Meter turned to 46 percent.

"Thank you for coming, Rivales!" Mr. Vance cried dramatically. The Rivales didn't move a muscle. They were like synchronized rocks.

"Did someone switch them off?" a little girl whispered to her dad.

Mr. Vance announced, "And the third and final video is from . . . the Talaskas!"

"Here it comes," Imo said. She sounded panicky about being up on the big screen. She added, "I'm sorry, Cal. Especially because watching Leslie boss Alison around has changed my mind about things."

Sorry? Why are you sorry? Cal almost asked. But he didn't want to miss a thing.

The world around Cal seemed to slow down, and his heart pounded. Mrs. T. must have known he was about to burst. She put a hand on his shoulder. "Easy."

Cal couldn't wait for everyone to see the video of his perfect family shopping like experts. Instead, something completely different appeared on the screen.

His ears reacted first.

"What's . . . with the . . . extra *P*!" Cal heard his mom say in the video. Then Mr. T. said, "Let it flow! Set it *free*!" When he heard Imo say, "What rhymes with *free*, Dad? It starts with a *P*!" Cal started feeling queasy.

Still, it took a second for him to figure out what he was looking at. He and his family were in a heap on the muddy ground in their backyard, a giant pile of arms, legs, a tail, and six laughing heads.

Then Cal heard himself say, "The Butler did it!" He saw the expression on his own face in the video—and his wet pants.

"What am I doing?" Cal asked out loud.

Mr. Carmody overheard him. "Hmm," he considered. "I'd say you're trying not to pee your pants. And I'm not sure you're succeeding."

For twenty seconds, the video showed the Talaskas laughing their heads off. Then, without warning, the screen went blank.

Once again, the audience was stunned. This time, not even Mr. Vance could recover. The Talaskas were frozen. Cal felt his face burning with embarrassment. The Audience Love Meter sat at 0 percent.

Leslie gave Cal a nasty smile and chuckled. The microphone picked up her laughter, and it went out to the crowd.

The sound was like a stick of dynamite blowing up a dam.

As if they had been waiting for the okay, people opened their mouths, and a flood of laughter and clapping filled the air.

Then the Audience Love Meter arrow shot up to 45 percent.

People were smacking each other's backs and reliving the video.

"What's with the extra *P*?" howled John Salmona, who lived down the street from the Talaskas. "Set it *free!*"

Next to John, Ms. Graves dabbed her wet eyes. "Holy moly," she said in a most unteacherly way. "The Butler did it! That's just awesome!"

"What's happening, Dad?" Cal asked. "Did they like it?"

"I'm not sure what's with all the racket," Mr. T. said. "But laughing is like a cold—you can catch it."

And it was true. The noise of laughter only grew. The dial on the Audience Love Meter raced to 70 percent. Cal could see Leslie looking around furiously. Even Mr. Wylot was starting to get worried. When the arrow approached the Wylots' score of 72, he grabbed the microphone.

"All right, all right, I think that's enough," Mr. Wylot said, putting up a hand. "Let's all calm down."

The crowd's laughter died down to chuckles, and Mr. Vance took the microphone back. "Well, that was something," he said. "Looks like we have our two finalist families! The Wylots and the Talaskas!"

Cal launched into the air and pumped his fist. "That's me!" he yelled at the top of his lungs.

"That's *us*!" Imo yelled even louder. She sounded as excited as he was to have won. Mr. and Mrs. T. didn't seem nearly as happy. Cal knew they had thought the video round would be the end of the contest for them.

"We'll see both families at the brand-new Wish Shoppe in two weeks, at nine AM sharp," Mr. Vance said over the hubbub. "If either the Wylots or the Talaskas fail to show up for the Great Grab, the Rivales will take their slot. So be on time! Remember, there will only be one winning family that day. One family will be allowed to keep everything they grab and will appear in our national ad. Stay tuned for more!"

Mr. Wylot did not look pleased. But he had a fake smile on his face and clapped. "Everyone is free to *grab* a plate and eat now! Enjoy!"

The velvet ropes were moved and the crowd stampeded to the barbecues, with the Rivales and Mr. Vance rushing to the head of the line.

"Not you, Mr. Vance," Mr. Wylot said. "I want to have a word with you."

He pulled Mr. Vance through the patio door into the house.

As his heartbeat slowed down, Cal's brain had a chance to catch up with what had just happened. He knew Wish Shoppe planned to put the winning videos online and on its billboards. The whole state . . . maybe the whole world . . . would see them.

"Why did you send that part of the video, Imo?" Cal asked. "I thought you were going to edit it."

"Sorry, there wasn't time." Imo shrugged. "In my opinion, though, it showed our family at our best. And it worked."

Cal wasn't so sure. He looked around, expecting to

find Leslie Wylot sneering at him. But the Wylots had already gone inside, as if bored with the company.

Cal wanted his family to win the contest so they could get whatever they'd like. But he also wanted the world to know that the Talaskas were the perfect family. Rolling around in the mud might not be the best way to show that.

Still, Imo had a point. The video had worked, and the Talaskas were finalists. They were going to the third round of the Wish Shoppe Great Grab Contest!

With the naming of the two finalist families, the small town of Hawkins exploded with Great Grab fever.

A few junior high kids who lived down the street rolled on the ground every time Cal went by on his bike. The kids acted like they were laughing so hard, they were about to pee their pants. As Cal pedaled away, they would call after him, "The Butler did it!" Cal had to admit it was kind of funny.

Still, something bothered him. He wasn't sure if their video had succeeded because people thought it was great—or because it was just a big joke.

Neighbors dropped off Wish Shoppe catalogs to give the Talaskas ideas for what to grab when they ran through the store. Jenny Vincent, a six-year-old from Brightmore Road, thought Cal should grab a life-sized ceramic ostrich. Other people circled sports equipment, jewelry, and car mats.

Dan MacGuire, an eighth grader from across the street, stopped Cal on the sidewalk. He'd drawn a star next to a roller coaster in a travel magazine.

Cal said, "Uh . . . I don't think that ride would fit in a shopping cart, Dan. Unless the cart was the size of Detroit."

"Yeah, but imagine the fun I can have—" Dan said, and then stopped. "Did I say *I*?" he asked, flustered. "I mean *you*! *You* as in *me*!" Finally, he gave up and said, "The Butler did it!"

Not everyone was as open about giving them ideas. When they stopped at Moylan's Gas Station, Mrs. Moylan left a note under one of the Flying Monkey's windshield wipers. The Talaskas found it when they got home. It read, "Get yourselves a new car! And thank you for standing up to them." By *them*, Cal knew Mrs. Moylan meant the Wylots.

Other people were nervous about openly rooting against the Wylots, too. The twin Weber girls snuck up to Mr. and Mrs. T. outside the library. Looking around as if the Wylots might see them, the twins gave them a list of lawn mowers.

While some of the ideas were pretty amazing, Cal still had his sights set on the Wonder World Video Game System. He'd be able to control the world around him! And owning a game that usually only hotels could afford would be a great way to prove how special the Talaskas were.

At school, Ms. Graves wrote LESLIE, IMO, and CAL on the board under the word CONGRATULATIONS!

"As your oh-so-hip English teacher, I'm not a fan of the old-world spelling of *Wish Shoppe*," Ms. Graves said. "But I'm very proud of the contest finalists in our class!" The rest of the students clapped, and the three took bows.

Imo and Cal managed to keep their distance from Leslie, and they just ignored any nasty comments she sent their way. Which wasn't always easy. Leslie had taped two sheets of paper on the wall outside the cafeteria. One was labeled TALASKA FANS at the top, and the other read WYLOT FANS. Leslie had been using scare tactics to get kids to sign the Wylot page.

So Cal was surprised when they came out of English class to find the Talaska Fans page completely filled in. Names scrawled in bright-purple ink covered the paper.

"Who signed this?" Leslie demanded angrily.

Cal stepped closer to see, and he laughed. "Some very important people."

"Like who?" Leslie snapped. "Wait until I mention them to my father."

"You should do that," Cal said. "I think George Washington, Teddy Roosevelt, and Abraham Lincoln will be very sorry."

"What does *that* mean?" Leslie peered at the Talaska page and snorted when she saw the names. They belonged to all the U.S. presidents and Canadian prime ministers. Leslie tore the sheets off the wall and stomped into the cafeteria, shouting for Alison to follow her.

"Who would dare do this, my fellow Americans?" James asked, perfectly copying the voice of the current president.

"Maybe the Butler did it?" Alison answered with a wink. She stuck her hands in her pockets and rushed after Leslie, but not before Cal saw the purple ink stains on her fingers.

That night, Cal called Grandma Gigi for the third time to tell her the amazing news about being contest finalists. She lived thirty minutes away. He got her answering machine again.

"I'm out and about, but leave me a shout," Gigi's greeting said. "And I'll call you back, without a doubt." Not the best poetry, Cal thought, but it was a clue as to why his dad rhymed when he got excited or nervous.

Even so, the good news kept coming. Ms. Donegan, who owned the Donegan Diner, had started dating James's dad. James helped out there for a couple of hours a week. He called to tell Cal that Ms. Donegan had created two new sandwiches in honor of the Wylots and the Talaskas.

Perfect timing. Cal's family needed all the encouragement they could get to keep going with the contest. Especially his parents.

Mrs. T.'s business was suddenly in trouble. The Olympic swimmer, the diver, and the linebacker who were supposed to speak at Wylot Auditorium next month all canceled on her. The athletes gave fake-sounding excuses, like still being dizzy from changing to daylight saving time or having a sick goldfish. Mrs. T. had already sold tickets to the events, and she would lose a ton of money when she had to send refunds.

Cal had an itchy feeling that Mr. Wylot was behind the athletes' not showing up. "It's called *Wylot* Auditorium, after all," he told his mom.

"No one is that awful," Mrs. T. said. Then, after thinking about it, she added, "But it is true that Mr. Wylot has been tough on your dad since that video elimination."

Saying *tough* in this situation was like saying the sun was *slightly warm*. Mr. Wylot was making Cal's dad's job at the factory almost impossible. Without warning, Mr. Wylot had taken away Mr. T.'s office. Now Cal's dad was stuck sitting in the hallway at a desk smaller than Cal's at school.

What did all this add up to?

Mr. and Mrs. T. were even less excited about the Great Grab Contest than before. "It's been kind of fun, Cal," Mrs. T. had said. "But we need to keep our eyes on real life and real jobs for a while."

That did not sound like a good plan to Cal.

A sandwich named after them could be just what they needed to get back on track! Cal convinced his family to head down to the diner for lunch, and the Talaskas hopped in the Flying Monkey. They drove to Main Street and parked close to the diner.

A chalkboard menu in front of the diner announced:

Come on in and try a . . .

Wylots' Maximum Force
or
Talaskas' The Butler Did It!

They're both a wish come true. . . .
Grab a great one TODAY!

"We're famous!" Cal said. "Come on, let's try a Talaska!"

"Those sandwiches are eight bucks," Mr. T. said. "We're not the Moneybag family, buddy."

"I got this one," Cal said, shaking his piggy bank, which he had brought from home. It sounded a little lighter than he remembered. "Well, we might have to split it, but it will be fun. Come on."

As the Talaskas went into the diner, Alison Mangan's dad walked out. Cal said hello, and Mr. Mangan nodded. From outside the big window, Mr. Mangan watched the Talaskas and quickly pulled out his cell phone before heading down the street.

Cal looked for James, but he was out with Ms. Donegan in the food truck. The Talaskas did run into the MacGuires, who yelled, "Why, hello!" as if real heroes had just entered the diner. And there was Mrs. Moylan sitting at the counter. She shook Mr. and Mrs. T.'s hands, smiling and wishing them luck with the contest. She didn't seem worried about supporting them now.

A few minutes later, the Talaskas took a seat in a booth, and a waitress came to take their order. Her name tag read MELINDA.

"We'll have five Talaskas, please," Cal said, counting his change on the table. "No, wait. Better make that *three* Talaskas, please."

"Talaska? What's that?" Melinda asked in a bored voice. "I don't think we have that."

Mrs. T. smiled. "We're friends of Ms. Donegan's," she said. "She named a sandwich after us. It's out on the sign."

Melinda leaned back to look outside. "I don't see that, sweetie," she said. Cal half stood so he could see the sign. And it was true—someone had wiped the name of the Talaska sandwich off the board.

Then he saw a man walking up to their table, clapping his hands together and sending clouds of chalk dust into the air. Cal could guess whom Mr. Mangan had been calling in such a hurry.

Mr. Wylot.

"Hello, Nelson," Mr. Wylot said to Cal's dad. He was a little out of breath, like he had hustled over to the restaurant. "I see you have time for lunch, but not work."

"It's Saturday—" Mr. T. started to say.

"Oh, Nelson, I'm just joking," Mr. Wylot said. He put his chalky hands on the table. "In fact, I'm here with good news that couldn't wait until Monday. I'm giving you a job in the new plant we're building on the out-skirts of the Mojave Desert."

Cal gasped, and Imo sputtered, "What?"

People at other tables looked their way.

"I was inspired to make the decision by something my beautiful daughter Leslie told me," Mr. Wylot said, and winked at Cal. "The job is scheduled to start imme-diately. I have a ten-year contract right here." He took a stack of papers out of his shoulder bag and smacked them down on the table. "Nelson Talaska, this contract will keep you in accounting for the rest of your life! Isn't that amazing?"

Mr. Wylot spoke loudly, as if he was showing off. A few other diners clapped lamely.

"Dad, say something," Cal said.

Mr. T. wouldn't look at him. Still, something changed in his face. "Mr. Wylot, this is too much," he said quietly. "That's something my family and I would have to think about and such."

Mr. Wylot smiled down on him. "There's nothing to think about. The job starts in three days. Until then, don't bother coming back to the factory here. Your work in Hawkins is over."

Cal couldn't take it. He asked his mom and dad, "But what about our house? James? Our other friends? The town?"

Bug barked. Imo guessed who he was talking about. "Yes," she said. "What about Sarah?"

"Who's Sarah?" Mr. Wylot asked.

"Our babysitter," Mrs. T. said.

"Hmm, I know Sarah," Mr. Wylot said. "Here's a fun fact. Did you know her college scholarship comes from the Wylot Foundation?"

"Wait," Cal said. "Do you mean she might get kicked out of school if we don't leave?"

"I never said that!" Mr. Wylot pretended to be

shocked. "Only that I control who gets money to pay for college. But let's talk about happier things, like your big move to the Mojave Desert."

This was all too much. Cal was dazed. "What about the contest?"

"What contest?" Mr. Wylot asked innocently. "Oh! You mean the Wish Shoppe Great Grab Contest? I'd forgotten all about that. I guess you'll miss out."

"Why are you doing this?" Cal asked, his face burning again, but this time because he was angry.

"Cal . . . ," his mom warned.

"No, let the boy ask," Mr. Wylot said. And he patted Cal on the head. "Do you know what a boss is?"

"I'm eleven, sir," Cal said.

"Good," Mr. Wylot said. "Then you know a boss is in charge. What would happen if the people who worked for him were suddenly beating him at contests? And everyone was watching, just as they are right now?" He gestured toward the other tables. "That wouldn't make him the boss anymore, would it?"

Cal got it. That was why Mr. Wylot was doing all this now at the diner. He wanted everyone in town to know he was running the show. And it was working. The faces of the few people who were still looking their way seemed to have changed. The hope Cal had seen in Mrs. Moylan's face had faded.

Mr. Wylot's smile was gone, too. His eyes burned like lasers into the Talaskas. Bug growled. Then Mr. Wylot clapped and waved over the waitress.

"Melinda, bring these folks a Wylot sandwich," he said. "They need the best in the house. And that's always a Wylot!"

Cal felt like a volcano that was about to blow. He struggled not to explode as his dad drove them home to Piedmont Place.

As the Flying Monkey pulled into the driveway, Cal saw the mailman trotting away down the sidewalk. The mailman spotted Cal and put his hands over his ears, singing "La la la" as if to block out anything Cal might say. Cal knew he was only half kidding. Cal had once persuaded him to do the chicken dance while delivering the mail.

As the family went into the house, they found a slip on the front door that the mailman had left. It said the Talaskas had a package waiting for them at the post office. Mrs. T. shouted after the mailman, "Thanks, Henry!"

In the kitchen, Butler and Bug had their spectacular reunion. If they were separated for more than three minutes, it was as if they'd been apart for weeks. Butler rolled on his back and wiggled, crying happily, and Bug did the same.

Finally, Cal couldn't keep it in anymore. "We CANNOT move to the Mojave Desert!" he blurted out. "How can that even be an option?"

At the kitchen counter, Mrs. T. was opening the gallon of chocolate ice cream they had picked up on the way home. She took bowls out of the cupboard, but no one seemed interested in ice cream. The contract from Mr. Wylot sat in front of Mr. T. on the table, blocking the spot where Cal's dad played his invisible keyboard.

"You're right, Cal, it's not an option at this time," Mr. T. said, flipping through the contract. "Mr. Wylot's new factory will be a couple hundred yards from the actual desert line."

"Dad!" Cal shouted. How could Mr. T. joke about this? Imo was watching everything, but she wasn't helping, either.

"This could be an opportunity for us, Cal," Mrs. T. said. "Life might be easier for everyone this way."

"But we'd still be under Mr. Wylot's thumb, just really . . . hot." Cal didn't know what to say or where to start. What about their house? They'd have to leave it.

Guessing what Cal was thinking, Mrs. T. said, "Yes, we'd have to leave this house and Hawkins."

Her face seemed to droop like she couldn't believe what she'd just said. And the rest of the family was quiet for a minute, too.

It was Imo who spoke first. "I'm with Cal on this one," she said. "In my opinion, this stuff *does* matter. What the Wylots are doing is just way too . . ."

"Unfair!" Cal cried.

"Exactly," Imo agreed. "It's as unfair as when Lando Calrissian tricked Han Solo in Cloud City!"

"Nothing's been decided," Mr. T. said. "I told Mr. Wylot we needed more time than he's provided."

If only we had a real piano, Cal thought. His dad would be able to play, and that would let him think. He would see how bad this moving idea was. They needed the Great Grab more than ever.

"Can't we wait until after the contest?" Cal asked.

Mrs. T. turned away to put the ice cream in the freezer. "Cal, this is way more important than some contest."

"This isn't just any contest," Cal said.

His dad held up his hands. "Okay, I can see how you kids feel," he said. "I'll wait to sign the contract as long as I can. Deal?"

Cal knew it was probably just to get him to stop arguing, but he'd take it for now. "Thanks, Dad."

★ ★ ★

Later that afternoon, Cal was doing homework on his bed. Or trying to. He couldn't keep his mind on algebra.

Why were his parents giving up so easily? It was driving him crazy. He needed to do something. He rushed to the phone. He made three calls and sent three emails about what was going on, all to the same person—Grandma Gigi.

Gigi was famous for being slow to respond to messages. She liked to think about what to say. Cal thought of the time he'd sent her a silly joke about a giraffe on a train. He waited for her to email back. She did. But three weeks later and with only one word: *ha*.

Today, luckily, she didn't take as long to get back to

him. He checked his email and found that she had written more than one word this time. There were two.

Cal thought of the slip the mailman had left on their front door. He jumped to his feet and ran to his bike in the garage. Imo was there, staring into space and tugging one ear. She had started to clean her wrenches but stopped. She was as distracted as he was.

"Where are you going?" she asked. "If it's to do something about all this, count me in. People like Mrs. Moylan and Alison Mangan need us to stand up to the Wylots!"

"All right, you can come," he said. "But hurry."

She hopped on her bike, and together they pedaled down Piedmont Place.

"Where are we going, anyway?" Imo asked.

Cal answered using the two words from Gigi's email: "Post office."

★ ★ ★

An hour later, Mr. and Mrs. T. were waiting on the front steps as Cal and Imo pedaled into the driveway. Mrs. T. had the phone in her hand and was talking to one of the neighbors.

"They're back, Denise," Mrs. T. said into the phone. "Thanks. I'll call you later."

"Looks like we made the wrong call," Mr. T. said. "The Wylots didn't kidnap them after all."

Cal was alarmed. "Is that what you thought?"

"We were kidding with each other," Mrs. T. said with a shrug. "Kind of. Anyway—" She shook her head, getting back on track. "Where were you?"

"At the post office," Cal said.

"Why?" Mrs. T. asked as Butler and Bug circled Imo and Cal, bouncing up and down. "Let's go inside and you can explain."

A minute later, they were settled around the kitchen table. The contract from Mr. Wylot sat at one end and they huddled at the other, like it was an animal that might bite them.

Mrs. T. put her hands on the table. "Look, guys," she said. "I know you're upset about the contest and everything."

"But you can't go that far without telling us," Mr. T. chimed in. Cal knew scolding them was hard for him. He hated being the adult. "You're creating too much fuss."

Imo and Cal both nodded, and Cal said, "Grandma Gigi sent us things she's been holding on to. Things to help."

Mrs. T.'s eyebrows went up. "Help do what? Your grandmother doesn't keep anything."

"She did," Cal said. "She has things for both of you." He put a cardboard box on the table. "There was a note inside saying we should give them to you now."

Mr. T. opened the flaps of the box. He reached inside and took out a limp piece of fabric. He peered at it. "Is that . . . ?" he asked.

Mrs. T.'s hand covered her mouth. "Oh," she said softly.

It was a faded yellow sweatband.

"There's a school yearbook in the box, too, Mom," Imo said. "We looked at it. You were the best athlete at our school . . . in the state . . . in almost every single sport."

"That's why you're always looking at the old school trophies," Cal said.

Mrs. T. nodded. "This was my lucky sweatband. No

one could stop me when I wore this." She took the band carefully out of Mr. T.'s hand, as if she couldn't believe it was real. She gave the faded material a little stretch. "I guess I've gotten a little out of shape since then."

Mr. T. touched her arm. "I think you're beautiful, no matter what."

"Thanks, honey." Mrs. T. wiped a tear off her cheek and stared at the sweatband.

"Gigi kept something for you, too, Dad," Imo said. She picked up a plastic box with his name on it and held it out to him. Through the clear lid, they could see a fancy pen.

"That's . . . that's the pen my uncle gave me for my high school graduation," he said. "I wasn't going to open the box until I signed my first big music contract."

"What else does Gigi's note say?" Mrs. T. asked.

"Nothing, really," Cal said. "Just that no one messes with this family."

"No one has 'messed' with the family," Mr. T. said. "I wouldn't let that be—" He stopped. His eyes took on a new spark.

"I'm wrong," he said. "Mr. Wylot has taken our jobs. Made our friends' lives difficult. That family has laughed at us and stolen our sandwich. This is where it ends."

He opened the plastic box and took out the pen. Cal thought he looked like a future king pulling a sword from a stone.

"Dad," Imo said, "the ink might not work after all these years."

Mr. T. smiled. "One way to find out. No more doubts."

"Rabbo!" Butler and Bug both barked from beneath the table. They must have been there the whole time.

Mr. T. pulled Mr. Wylot's contract closer. He uncapped the pen and held it to the paper. He looked at them with his glasses slanted on his face. "No one messes with my family."

As his pen scratched across the contract, writing *NO DEAL*, Mrs. T. slid the sweatband onto her head. *BAM!* It was as if she grew a foot taller. She picked up Mr. Wylot's contract and tore it into small bits.

Mrs. T. looked at each of them and then said in a strong, clear voice, "We have to win this contest."

The rules of the Great Grab were clear.

Mr. Vance called to make sure the Talaskas knew to be at the brand-new Wish Shoppe in seven days, at exactly nine AM. They and the Wylots would be the first visitors allowed in the Wish Shoppe. Until then, both families were to keep clear of the store, even the parking lot.

"We don't want anyone getting an unfair advantage," Mr. Vance said. For some reason, the Vice President of Fun sounded less perky than usual. "You must also agree to the legal document I just emailed you. Don't be scared of words like *death by shopping cart, hopelessly marooned,* or *mysterious vomiting.* The document is for everyone's good and super fun!"

Before Mr. Vance hung up, he reminded them there would be a final elimination round on the day of the contest. Only one family would be allowed to keep everything they could grab in the store.

"How will they make the decision?" Imo wondered out loud after Mr. Vance's call. Cal was sitting with her and their mom in the living room. Mr. T. was out back with Butler and Bug.

"Good question," Mrs. T. said. She had put the headband away for now and was perched in front of her computer. "These contests always have some kind of wild twist."

"Then we better get set for anything they can throw at us," Cal said. "The good thing about you and Dad not having work is that we can train for the contest."

"That's the only good thing," Mrs. T. said. She glanced at the stack of bills next to her keyboard.

"We just have to make it for another week, until the Great Grab," Cal assured her.

Mrs. T. didn't seem convinced. But maybe she saw the worry on Cal's face, because she said, "You could be right."

To change the subject, Mrs. T. tapped her computer screen. "I did a quick search on the Wish Shoppe," she said. "Check out this news story."

Cal and Imo leaned in to read it.

Michigan Teen Lost in Wish Shoppe for Three Days
By Park Ridgefield for the *Hawkins Herald*

Alex Dante, thirteen, of Grand Rapids has been found after going missing on April 22. Alex had last been seen near the entrance of the Wish Shoppe Circles of Dreams in East Lansing, Michigan.

"I dropped Alex off at the bridge that leads across that River of Low Prices," his mother told this reporter. "By the time I parked the car, he was gone."

Alex vanished without a trace. For three days, his parents and friends searched the area around the store. All with no luck. No one guessed that Alex was actually *inside* the store the whole time.

"I got lost in the Clothing Circle," Alex said after being rescued by an equally lost eighty-five-year-old woman looking for garbanzo beans. "I wandered into the Appliance Circle. I made a tent out of a big cardboard box and drank water from a floor-sample refrigerator. My biggest wish was to get out of Wish!"

How could a straight-A junior high school student get lost in a store for three days? Simple. All fifty Wish Shoppes are jammed with five acres of every kind of product on the planet. Shoppers complain that there is no rhyme or reason to the stores. Aisles branch out from different departments—or Circles of Dreams—and lead nowhere or spiral into dead ends.

The founder of the stores, King Wonder, has often said, "Wishes can lead you anywhere! So our Wish Shoppes have Circles of Dreams and aisles that lead to other Circles and aisles and so on and so on and on and on and on. What's so confusing about that?"

Cal had read enough. "Okay, that can't be true!" he said. "The writer's totally making that up! We would have heard about that kid getting lost."

"Maybe King Wonder is covering it up," Imo said. She leaned closer to the computer. "The rest of the article says Alex and the eighty-five-year-old got lost again. They had to be re-rescued by a toddler who stumbled into the Appliance Circle."

"A toddler wandering the store alone?" Cal rolled his eyes. "Come on!"

Imo shrugged. "Could be true. All those Circles and aisles make a pretty confusing maze. I mean, have you ever been in one of those stores?"

"Uh, yes," Cal answered. "Maybe three or four times . . . *with you*."

"And how many of those times did we get lost?" Imo countered. "Three or four?"

Secretly, Cal admitted Imo had a point. "I still think that story's a lie."

"Just because *you* make everything up doesn't mean other people do," Imo fired back.

Mrs. T. held up her hands. "Okay, okay. It doesn't matter if this stuff is true. We just need to figure out a path through the store that will take us to the things we want."

"I'm on it," Cal said. He ran up to his bedroom, grabbed his whiteboard, and brought it back to the living room. The board was where Cal came up with some of his best ideas—like the master plan to convince his parents they needed a swimming pool. (That plan had failed in the first stage: "Persuade parents to wear sweaters during a heat wave so they get really, really hot.")

Cal uncapped his marker and got ready to write down ideas from Mrs. T. "Okay, shoot," he said.

Now that his parents were on board with the contest, Cal figured he would have to give up a little control. But his mom shook her head.

"We'll all come up with ideas," Mrs. T. said. "But mostly it's got to be you, Cal. Think of your dad and me as the team owners, and you're the quarterback. Okay?"

"Better than okay," Cal said. "Thanks, Mom."

Imo didn't seem as enthusiastic about this way of thinking. But she finally nodded. "All right, all right," she groaned. "What should we do first, oh, mighty QB?"

Cal wrote one word on the board: MAP.

Because they weren't allowed to visit the store before the contest and they couldn't find a map of it online, Cal came up with a plan to make their own map. That way, they could plot their course.

He asked Mrs. T. to hunt for pictures online from other Wish Shoppes—and she found quite a few. Most were of people goofing around, holding up a compass or scratching their heads as if hopelessly lost. A few held up wish lists that included things like "I wish I could find my way out of here!" Mrs. T. printed out the photos, and the family pieced them together into a weird kind of map.

Imo and Cal taped it to the living room wall and stood back to take a look.

"Holy Aristotle," Cal breathed. "That map is huge."

"Just like the store," Mrs. T. said. "After all, it covers more land than downtown Hawkins."

To train their brains to find what they wanted, Cal asked Imo to invent scavenger hunts around the house. He timed family members as they darted in and out of rooms, up and down stairs, looking for the strange items on Imo's lists.

"Here, Dad," Imo said, and handed Mr. T. a checklist. "You have to find old floss, a green feather, and a toy army figure."

Cal was pretty athletic, but no one in the family had ever prepped for a competition quite like this. They were sloppy at first, tripping over their own feet and panicking when time started to run out.

When Bug ran into Imo carrying a bucket of sand from the sandbox and it fell into the dishwasher, Cal was struck by a bad thought. The chaos would be three

million times worse at the Wish Shoppe. With so many amazing possibilities of things they could put in their carts—like toys, TVs, or tennis racquets—plus the time pressure, Cal realized they would be a mess.

"One thing," he said that night at the dinner table. The family was exhausted and just about to dig into Bug's second-favorite meal, meat loaf.

"What one thing?" Imo asked, pouring ketchup on her meat loaf.

"That's the answer," Cal said. "We need to stick with the *one thing* that each of us wants on the day of the contest. Otherwise we're going to get distracted and make mistakes. After we get that, we can grab whatever else we want if there's time."

"Excellent advice," Mr. T. said. When everyone agreed, he added, "Please pass the rice."

The next day, the family spent hours plotting routes on the map. They stuck with just the Circles that had things they wanted: gym equipment, musical instruments, science gear, video games, and . . . Bug still wasn't clear on what he wanted.

"We can forget about this whole side of the store," Cal said, pointing to the map. "All the Circles we want to hit, like the Fun and Games Circle and the Fitness Circle, are over here."

"But what if we get lost?" Imo said. "And wind up on the other side?"

"We won't," Cal said. "We're going to be too prepped for that."

Cal decided they should get ready for any possible tricks Mr. Vance might throw their way at the final elimination. Like doing everything backward, including talking.

"No emoc!" Cal said. "Nuf s'ti!"

Imo threw a couch pillow at him. "Bmud s'taht!"

They kept practicing, pretending to shop while skipping, singing, and spinning. The Talaskas trained all day, every day.

The night before the contest, Cal studied the map of the store . . . for what felt like the billionth time. He barely noticed that his dad was behind him and had his glasses on a slant.

Mr. T. was mumbling something about "memorizing the entire store." But Cal was too busy staring at the map and didn't really hear him. He focused on the Fun and Games Circle. That was where he would grab the

Wonder World Video Game System. Once Cal had that, he would toss into the cart anything else that would fit.

But there was one thing he dreamed of grabbing tomorrow more than anything—and that was respect. Cal wanted the Wylots and everyone else in Hawkins to treat his family like the winners he knew they were.

In fact, Cal wanted it so deeply, he imagined he could see the word *RESPECT* floating over the map.

"I'm coming for you," Cal said, tapping the map, and then he went to bed.

On the morning of the Great Grab Contest, the Talaskas woke up and brushed their teeth, as they always did. But Cal noticed something different.

There wasn't fighting over who was next in line for the bathroom. No frantic search for a missing sock. No BTAs. Cal's family was like a well-oiled machine.

We're just like the Rivales, he thought. Then Bug smeared toothpaste in Imo's hair, and Cal thought, *Well, not exactly.*

Cal, Imo, and Bug came downstairs to the kitchen, where their parents were waiting. Mr. T. started ringing the family bell like crazy.

"Surprise!" Mrs. T. said. "If we're going to be a strong

team today, we should look the part. Your dad and I made costumes!"

Mr. T. pointed to six piles of clothing on the table. Five of them had a purple velvet belt and a purple velvet shirt with a family member's name on the front and TALASKA on the back. There was even a new purple collar for Butler.

"Hmm," Cal said. Was this a good idea? But Imo had already pulled her shirt on top of her overalls, and Bug was putting the collar on Butler.

Why not? Cal thought. He slid the belt through the loops in his pants and reached for his shirt. It was baggy

in places and tight in others, but he loved it. He felt like a superhero.

"Thanks!" he said to his parents. "We've got forty-five minutes to get to the Wish Shoppe. Plenty of time, but we should hit the road right after we eat."

They wolfed down a breakfast of pancakes and, feeling pumped, hustled out to the driveway. But when they got there, it was as if someone let all the air out of their balloon.

Or tire.

"Oh no," Cal said.

The Flying Monkey's front-right tire had finally collapsed. The car was hunched over to one side, the tire rim resting on the gravel.

Imo crouched and touched the tire's gaping hole. "I can't patch it. The hole's too big. The Flying Monkey is grounded."

"And so are our hopes of getting to the Wish Shoppe on time," Mrs. T. groaned. Then her eyes went to Mr. T.'s face. "Honey, are you okay?"

As Cal watched, a vein on Mr. T.'s neck popped out and his cheek started twitching. Mr. T. opened his mouth, and Cal thought about when he poured soda too quickly into a glass—how the fizz would overflow and go everywhere. That seemed to be happening with his dad.

As Mr. T. stared at the deflated tire, he looked like everything inside him was about to overflow.

"Honey?" Mrs. T. said again.

Mr. T. clamped his mouth shut in a tight line. Then he stomped toward the house, counting to ten. Actually, he went way past ten and just kept going and going.

This can't be the way things end, Cal thought. His mind raced through possible solutions.

"We could walk," Cal said.

Imo shook her head. "Way too far."

"Bikes?"

Imo shook her head again. Cal remembered that their mom didn't have one and she couldn't ride double.

"Let's get a lift from someone," Cal said. As if on cue, a van started up in the driveway next door and backed into the street. It was the Rivales! *They must be heading out to the Wish Shoppe,* thought Cal.

"Wait!" he shouted. Waving his arms, he ran with Imo to the sidewalk. But the Rivales must have thought the Talaskas were just saying hello. They waved back in perfect unison and drove down the street.

Imo looked at the other houses. "Everyone else is gone!" she said miserably.

She was right. Cal thought about calling James's sister for a ride. But she didn't have a cell phone. And James and his dad were already at the Wish Shoppe with the Donegan Diner food truck. "Can we call a taxi?" Cal asked Mrs. T.

His mom smiled and shook her head. "This is Piedmont Place, honey!"

Cal kicked the ground. His mom was right. There wasn't a taxi within an hour of them. By then, the Talaskas would be disqualified from the contest and the Rivales would take their place.

"Rabbo!" Butler barked while spinning around and around. Bug joined in. "Rabbo! Rabbo! Rabbo!"

Cal turned to see what Butler and Bug were so excited about.

Holy Aristotle.

"Wait a second," Mr. T. said from near the house. His face looked almost calm again. "Is that a . . . ?"

"I think it is," Cal answered.

A car tire was rolling down Piedmont Place.

"What the provolone is going on?" Mrs. T. asked.

Like a homing pigeon, the tire angled toward the Talaskas' driveway, but it missed and bounced off the curb. The force sent it wobbling for a few more feet, and then it fell over.

Mr. T. trotted into the street and turned the tire upright. Imo joined him, and they rolled the tire to the Flying Monkey.

"Does it fit?" Cal asked.

Imo nodded, dumbfounded. "It's perfect, in my opinion. Where did this come from?"

That was when Cal noticed the writing along the inside rim of the tire. "The Butler did it!" had been scrawled in purple ink.

"Someone really wants us to make it to the Wish Shoppe," Cal said. "But who?"

No one had an answer, and the family had to get moving. *Right now!*

Imo and Mr. T. put on the new tire, and the Talaskas climbed into the Flying Monkey. When Mr. T. turned the key, the song "We Are Family" boomed out of the busted CD player. It had never sounded so good.

"Are we going to make it, Dad?" Imo asked.

Mr. T. nodded. But the way he gripped the steering wheel made it clear he wasn't sure.

When the Talaskas pulled into a parking space at the Wish Shoppe and poured out of the car, it was 8:58 AM. Two minutes to spare. The first thing Cal noticed was the hundreds of butterfly-shaped balloons that formed a wall between the parking lot and the store. They floated and flapped in the wind, tugging gently on the strings that tied them to the ground.

Three news vans and a crowd of about two hundred people, including the Wylots, the Rivales, and Mr. Vance, were already gathered next to the balloons.

Like the Talaskas, the Wylots were in costume. They had on the long fur coats from their video and wore bandanas around their necks. Cal and his family hustled over to them. Leslie glanced at her watch and frowned, clearly upset the Talaskas were on time.

Cal spotted James and his dad behind the Wylots. James and Cal exchanged thumbs-ups. "Go get 'em, Captain!" James called.

"Um, what's he doing here?" Leslie pointed at Butler. Bug stepped in front of him, as if trying to protect the dog from lightning that might fire out of her finger.

"Family members who were in the videos get to be in the contest," Cal said. He wasn't sure if that was a rule. He had just never thought about leaving Butler home.

Leslie opened her mouth to say something nasty or challenge him when—

Bug looked up into her eyes and softly barked, "Rabbo." He wrapped his arms around Butler's neck, and Butler pressed his head against Bug's.

"Aw, how adorable!" Mrs. MacGuire cooed from the crowd. Cal had to admit that it was pretty darn cute. And even Leslie couldn't resist.

She seemed torn. Finally, she held up her hands and said, "Whatever! Let Butler do it!"

"I thought the Butler already *did* it!" someone said, and the audience laughed.

Cal nodded his thanks to Leslie, who was already back to her usual nasty self. She rolled her eyes at Cal just as the butterfly balloons were pulled back like a curtain. They revealed something—no, make that *someone*—amazing. . . .

King Wonder!

The owner of Wish Shoppe was here, in the flesh. With a gold crown perched on his silver head, King sat

upon his Throne of Savings. The chair was made of giant dollar signs, and he waved a gold scepter with a butter-fly on top.

Mr. Vance tapped his shoulder, and King's dreamy eyes came into focus. "Oh good-good-good!" King said in a high-pitched voice. "Now we can begin!"

He waved to the news cameras, and they all pointed in his direction.

"Welcome, one and all!" King announced. "Welcome to the Great Grab Contest at the Wish Shoppe Circles of Dreams, where shopping is so easy, you'll forget where you are!"

There was a snicker or two from the audience. King

cleared his throat. "It's a beautiful day here along the River of Low Prices, the largest man-made river in the world!"

The "river" was six feet wide and three feet deep and ran all the way around the store. The water was clear, as in a swimming pool, and dollar signs had been painted along the bottom—as if high prices had tried getting into the store and sunk to the bottom instead.

Mr. Vance leaned in to whisper in King's ear. "Fine, fine . . . make that the largest man-made river in the general area!" King said. He smiled warmly at Mr. Vance. "What would we do without our trusty Vice President of Fun?"

Cal noticed that the Wylots grinned at each other.

"Our two finalist families, the Wylots and the . . ." King paused. "We're sorry, but we're having trouble saying this other name. . . ."

Why does King say we *when he's talking about himself?* Cal wanted to ask, but his dad responded before he could. "We're the Talaskas," Mr. T. said.

"It rhymes with *Nelson, you're fired,*" Mr. Wylot said, as if trying to be helpful.

"It does? Really?" King asked, appearing confused. Then he continued, "As you know, there will be one final elimination round, and only one family will get to keep what they grab today. At first, we thought we might ask a trivia question to eliminate one family. Maybe a question about the rarest purple flowering plant on the Apalachicola River."

"That's the Florida skullcap," Mrs. T. said instantly.

The crowd gasped as people checked her answer on their cell phones. "She's right," Maisy Franklin, the librarian, said in awe.

We won! Cal thought.

But King was still talking. "Then we decided no, no, no. We should do something physical. You know, really get the old blood pumping. Like walking on your hands for a hundred feet."

Bug flipped over. And darted around the concrete on his hands.

We won! Cal thought again.

"But . . . we thought no," King said. "That's not right, either. We figured it should be more interesting. We decided the elimination should happen *inside* the store *while* the Great Grab is taking place."

"Here comes the twist," Mrs. T. said.

King sat back and waved his scepter at Mr. Vance, a signal for him to take over.

"Thanks, King," Mr. Vance said. "Our shoppers know there are nine Circles of Dreams inside every Wish Shoppe. But do they know how to find them fast? To prove you're the perfect shoppers we love, you must visit each Circle in the store and take the ribbons with your family's name. You'll find them in the center of the Circles. You're not allowed to touch the other family's ribbons."

Panic seeped into Cal's body. And he could feel the rest of his family tense up, too. They had planned on going only to the Circles where they wanted things, not *all* the Circles in the store!

"Of course," Mr. Vance said with a chuckle, "you can grab whatever you'd like along the way and put it in your cart!"

When he said *cart*, two men in Wish Shoppe uniforms appeared, pushing two jumbo-sized shopping carts. They rolled one over to each family. Cal could see a digital timer, set to twenty minutes, stuck below the handle.

As Imo examined the cart, Mr. Vance asked her, "Are you excited, little girl?"

The cameras pointed at her, and Imo suddenly looked like one of the Rivales. Her face went blank and she froze.

"Awesome!" Mr. Vance said, as if Imo had just said something very interesting. He turned back to the other family members. "You have twenty minutes to grab what you want and get back to the starting point. Everything you grab must be in your cart, and everyone in your family has to cross the line together. If you don't return within twenty minutes with all nine Circle ribbons, you get nothing."

"Oh, and one last thing . . . ," King said with mischief in his eyes.

"Here comes another twist," Mrs. T. whispered. Cal braced himself.

"There is no talking allowed inside the store," King said with a wink. "If you speak, your family will be disqualified and you will lose." He took a breath and asked, "Are you ready to make all your wishes come true?"

"Yes!" Cal shouted, and the rest of the Talaskas nodded. The Wylots pulled their bandanas up over their faces, making them look like bank robbers. Their eyes bored into the Talaskas, and then they, too, nodded to King Wonder.

"Go grab your dreams!" King shouted.

A starter cannon fired and, after all the nuttiness of the past few weeks, the last round of the Great Grab Contest had finally begun!

With a loud *tick tick tick*, the timer on the Talaskas' cart started counting down from twenty minutes to zero.

"Let's go!" Mr. T. got behind the cart and pushed it. Or tried to. Maybe he shoved too hard, or maybe the cart was just ready to break. But the second Mr. T. put pressure on it, the cart toppled over.

"Whoa," Mrs. T. said.

Mr. T. flipped it back upright and tried again. The cart skittered onto its side. The crowd started chuckling.

"Do you need an instruction manual?" a teenager asked. The audience laughed again, and it stung Cal a little. People had already figured they were going to lose to the Wylots.

Ignoring the laughter, Imo spun the wheels of the flipped cart. "The wheels are fine, but the balance is all out of whack," she said. "If we push it, it will keep flipping."

"We need a new cart, Mr. Wonder!" Cal shouted.

King started to get to his feet, but Mr. Vance leaned in to whisper in his ear. Sitting back in the throne, King said, "You get only one cart."

"That's not fair!" Cal called back.

"Fair?" King asked, as if he had never heard of the word. "We're sorry, but those are the rules."

As the Talaskas stood looking down at their wounded shopping cart, the Wylots had already sped across the bridge over the River of Low Prices. Leslie glanced back and gave Cal a nasty wave as they disappeared into the store.

"This is a nightmare," Cal said.

The other Talaskas weren't listening. They were all talking at once and kept lifting the cart and trying to push it, but it just wouldn't stay upright.

"*Ting ting ting!*" Cal said, imitating their family bell, and they quieted down. "We can't panic, guys. It's just a matter of figuring it out, right, Imo?"

While Cal and Mrs. T. held the cart upright, Imo took a closer look.

"We can't push it," she said. "But that doesn't mean we can't pull it. We just need to do it from the right angle." She got down on her knees and pulled the front of the cart. It moved toward her smoothly with no sign of tipping over. "See, this works!"

"We can't crawl around the store in twenty minutes!" Cal said.

"Give me your belts," Imo said. "Quick!"

Without asking what she was up to, everyone slid off their purple belts and handed them over. Imo moved fast, like a one-girl pit crew at a NASCAR race. In thirty seconds, she had knotted their belts together into a small harness and tied it to the front of the cart.

"Come here, Bug," Imo said.

"I don't know, honey," Mrs. T. said, guessing what she was up to.

Imo shrugged. "We're too big for the harness, and so is Butler—but Bug isn't."

Bug stepped into the loop, and Imo tightened it snugly around his waist. "You okay?" Imo asked him.

Bug barked happily. And Cal knew why. He probably felt like a sled dog!

As if Butler had never been more proud, he barked, "Rabbo!"

Now that the Talaskas had a cart that barely worked *and* they had to visit all nine Circles in the store, Cal needed to come up with a new plan on the fly. "Okay, listen up," he said. "I'll grab the ribbon from the Television Circle on the way to the Fun and Games Circle. You guys get the ribbons from your Circles, and we'll meet at the Pet Circle, okay?"

Imo did the math in her head. "That leaves four ribbons."

"I know," Cal said. "They're on the other side of the store. The side we didn't study."

He held up a hand before she could say *And whose fault is that?*

"We'll have to grab the other ribbons after we meet at the Pet Circle," Cal said. "Bug, you'll pull the cart with Butler in one big loop around the store until you reach the Pet Circle, and we'll meet you there with what we grab. We can run faster if we're on our own. Okay?"

All agreed, and with that, the family was off and running across the River of Low Prices.

The glass doors of the Wish Shoppe slid open—

"Remember, no talking inside!" Cal warned them.

—and then the doors closed behind them with a *whoosh*.

In the future, a Well Wisher wearing butterfly wings would be waiting at the entrance to shout, "Welcome to Wish Shoppe, where your wishes come true!" Today, of course, it was as quiet and creepy as an empty school—a giant, seemingly endless school. Perky dentist-office music drifted down from the speakers. Cal imagined he could hear the rattle of the Wylots' cart somewhere in the acres of aisles and products.

And, of course, there was the ticking of the timer on the cart. They had already lost four minutes!

Cal held a finger up to his lips. *No talking, remember?*

he said to Bug with his face and eyes. And Bug made the same gesture to Butler, who twirled his tail in agreement.

But Imo was looking at Cal, not Bug or Butler—as if she knew that Cal would have an even tougher time with the no-talking rule. After all, talking was one of Cal's greatest talents.

The Talaskas stood in a circle, put their hands in the center, and pumped them up and down three times. They couldn't say it, but Cal knew they were all thinking it: *Talaskas together!*

Then, with one last wave from Mrs. T. to all of them, the Talaskas split up. Bug and Butler headed off along the outer wall. The rest of the family chose different aisles and dove into the heart of the store.

Cal sprinted toward the Fun and Games Circle. Or where he remembered it was from the map they'd made. It should be just past the Television Circle. His shoes slapped on the shiny tile as he raced past clay knick-knacks shaped like famous skyscrapers and through displays of canned peas. He was starting to get worried when a giant circular wall of TVs rose all around him.

Yes! The Television Circle!

The thousands of TVs had the sound turned off but

flickered with color. Some were tuned to the local TV station and showed King Wonder talking to the crowd outside.

The rest of the sets displayed Cal.

Wait . . . what?

As Cal ran by, he could see himself running on the screens—or at least his hair. Who was taking video of the top of his head? He looked up and spotted security cameras whizzing along tracks on the ceiling. The TVs showed what the cameras saw!

Distracted and still moving fast, Cal caught his foot on something and tripped. He opened his mouth to shout—and then, remembering the rules, clamped it shut again.

Somehow Cal got his balance before he wiped out. He looked back, trying to find what he had tripped on. And the answer was obvious.

A rope had been strung across the aisle, close to the ground. This was just the kind of thing Emma Wylot would do.

Little did she know she had done him a favor. The rope had forced Cal to slow down—and remember the ribbon! He would have kept running like a madman without getting it.

A purple ribbon with TALASKA printed in block letters sat on a glass table in the middle of the Circle. The Wylots must have taken theirs already. Cal stuffed the purple ribbon in his back pocket and kept moving.

He knew he was just seconds away from the next Circle and the Wonder World Video Game System!

When he arrived in the Fun and Games Circle, it was empty, but the air buzzed as if someone had just been there. Before Cal could forget again, he went to the center of the Circle and picked up the second Talaska ribbon.

Then he let himself take a good look around. Suddenly, his feet wanted to move in every direction at once. The shelves were filled with marvels such as robots that made lunch, smartphone earrings, hologram Ping-Pong, and a Clap-n-Gro plastic tree, which grew and danced when you clapped. It was dizzying, and Cal knew why people could get lost so easily. He wanted to GRAB it all, and he couldn't remember which direction he had come from.

This is what we trained for, Cal told himself. He closed

his eyes for one second to get a grip. It would cost precious time on the clock, but it was worth it.

Calmer now, Cal opened his eyes . . . and there!

How had he missed it before? A giant blinking sign under a shelf read:

WONDER WORLD VIDEO GAME SYSTEM!

But the shelf was empty.

Cal didn't panic. He searched the Circle until he spotted just the edge of a box dangling over a top shelf. It was a Wonder World Video Game System!

Someone—more than likely, someone with the last name Wylot—must have tossed all the Wonder Worlds up there. How was Cal going to get his hands on that one?

Tick tick tick. Cal didn't need the cart's timer in front of him to feel the seconds ticking down.

Should he give up on the Wonder World? Grab something else? What about that dancing plastic tree? It was pretty cool and all set to go—he just had to drag it to the Pet Circle and toss it in the cart.

No, Cal thought. He wasn't going to let the Wylots stop him from getting what he wanted.

Cal looked around for a ladder, a trampoline, or a giant pogo stick—anything that might help him reach the high shelf. Nothing. Just the toys, the electronics, and that drooping plastic tree.

Desperate, Cal started climbing the shelves. Not easy. Each shelf jutted out slightly over the one below it. Soon the angle made it almost impossible to hang on.

This wasn't working. He jumped to the ground with a thud.

Where was Bug? Cal could have used the shopping cart as a stepladder. No, he realized, it wasn't Bug he needed. It was Imo. Or at least he needed to think like Imo.

What would Imo do? She'd use the stuff around her like tools to solve the problem.

Cal's eyes darted around the Circle again. *Yes!*

He grabbed the Clap-n-Gro plastic tree in its pot and dragged it to a spot under the Wonder World.

He looped an arm around one of the top branches and started clapping. The tree rose slightly, lifting his feet off the ground. It was working! Cal kept clapping, and soon he was five feet in the air. He was nearly five feet tall himself, so he just might be able to stretch and reach the Wonder World.

But it was no good. Whenever he stopped clapping

to reach for the box, the tree would droop slightly and he'd drop down. Cal tried clapping with one hand. But that didn't work. He thought for a second.

Of course! With his arm still looped around the branch, he slapped his forehead a few times.

Whap! Whap! Whap!
Ow! Ow! Ow!

The tree didn't know the difference between his clapping his hands or his head. It danced and swayed to the rhythm. His feet slammed into the toys on the shelves below him. Boxes of electronic musical toys and calculators went flying.

Cal held on and stretched. . . .

His fingers grazed the Wonder World box. He grabbed one

end and pulled it toward the edge. It was too heavy, and gravity yanked it out of his hand. The box fell end over end and hit the floor with a plastic-crunching crack!

Uh-oh. That didn't sound good.

Cal could be next—only it wouldn't be plastic that would crack.

"Greetings, dearest Wish Shoppe shoppers!" King Wonder's voice boomed over the speaker system. "We wish to let you know that time is flowing quickly. You have thirteen minutes left to fill your carts with dreams and ribbons, and return to the finish line!"

Cal didn't have time for another clapfest with his forehead. He had to keep moving.

He made a quick decision. Cal eased up on the slapping, and it was like lifting his foot off the pedal of a go-kart. The tree ran out of gas. The dancing stopped, and it slowly drooped toward the floor.

Halfway down, Cal let go of the branch, and he landed on the hard tiles. He grabbed the box at his feet and started running.

With the box clutched under one arm, he sprinted out of the Circle and down an aisle of Styrofoam coolers and beach umbrellas. He was sure it led to the Pet

Circle. But he was wrong. He suddenly found himself facing the outermost wall of the store.

As the seconds ticked away, Cal struggled to remember the details on the map.

Which way should he go?

And where was that mooing coming from?

M^{oo!}

Baa!

Cock-a-doodle-doo!

Animal sounds came from the next aisle. On a hunch, Cal followed the noises. He wasn't sure what to expect when he came around the corner, but it definitely wasn't what he found.

Hundreds of stuffed toys shaped like a farmer were scattered in a knee-high heap on the floor. And in the center of them all were Butler and Bug. Cal's brother was still in his harness and struggling to pull the cart through the heap. Butler's paws were digging at the toys like he was trying to create a path for Bug.

Cal recognized the Friendly Farmer toys from TV

ads. They were supposed to help little kids learn about animals.

A giant canister filled with Friendly Farmers had collapsed on top of Bug and the cart. It was as if Bug were stuck in a ball pit, but instead of balls there were chattering farmers, complete with straw hats and pitchforks. The farmers' touch screens must have clicked on when they fell, because they were all making strange farm noises.

The cows' mooing was so weirdly high-pitched, it hurt Cal's ears. And the chickens' clucking reminded him of a teakettle at full blast.

Cal had to hand it to Bug and Butler. They weren't freaking out. They were just determined to get loose. Butler started clamping down on the toys with his mouth and throwing them to the side. Bug tried to pull the cart free, but there were just too many of them. Cal waded through the toys, throwing aside each squawking, cackling, quacking farmer, until he reached Bug.

Cal gave Butler a quick scratch, and then he put his hands out as if asking, *What happened?*

Bug's lips parted to say something. Then, remembering the silence rule, he used his face and hands to say, *I don't know!*

Cal almost laughed. For the first time, talking with Bug actually made sense!

Under all the toys, Cal discovered that a rope had been strung across the aisle, just as in the Television Circle. One end was tied to the canister that had been overflowing with Friendly Farmer toys. Bug and Butler had tripped on the rope, and the canister had fallen over.

Cal had zero doubt this was another trap set by the Wylots. Why were they more concerned with stopping the Talaskas than with getting stuff in their cart?

In a flash, Cal realized the answer: The Wylots didn't care about getting more things today. They already had all the expensive junk they could ever wish for. They wanted to grab the one thing they couldn't put in their cart: to win at any cost and show the town and the world that they were the boss.

Right now, the Wylots were scattered throughout the store, making sure of just that. They were probably setting other traps. *If only I could see what they were up to,* Cal thought as a security camera whizzed overhead.

But, of course, he could. He knew what he had to do.

Cal, Bug, and Butler finished clearing away the Friendly Farmers—except for one that Butler kept in his mouth. Cal tossed the box he'd grabbed in the Fun and Games Circle into the cart. The weight of the box restored the cart's balance. Cal could now push it without tipping it over.

Bug shook his head and pointed at himself. *No, I want to pull!* Then he opened his mouth as if he would yell if he didn't get his way.

Cal held up his hands. This wasn't the time for a BTA. *Fine! Knock yourself out! But go this way! We're making a detour.* Cal jabbed his finger toward where he had just come from.

Bug and Butler took off. Cal hustled to keep up. He reached them just in time to stop them at the Television Circle.

Many of the TVs still showed what was happening

outside the store. But that wasn't why Cal had wanted to come back here. His eyes searched for the TVs tuned to the security cameras.

Bug pointed at a TV above Cal's head. *Mom!* Bug mouthed silently.

Cal followed his brother's finger to the screen. It showed Mrs. T. in the Fitness Circle. She was sweating and taking a moment to catch her breath.

From this angle, Cal could see someone his mom couldn't.

Mrs. Wylot.

Leslie's mom was on the other side of the Fitness Circle. As Cal and Bug watched helplessly, Mrs. Wylot took down a sign that read THIS WAY TO THE PET CIRCLE! and replaced it with one that said THIS WAY CLOSED!

When Mrs. T. tried to meet up with the rest of the Talaskas, she would get hopelessly lost!

Pulling Cal's arm, Bug pointed at another TV. *Imo!*

Imo was in the Hardware Circle. Why was she just standing there? Cal looked more closely. She was straining to move, but her feet were stuck to the ground. Literally.

As ridiculous as it seemed, Imo had stepped into a pool of glue that companies used to make furniture.

It poured out of a bucket that had been tipped over on the floor. Cal felt like he was watching a cartoon. But this was all too real. Even if Imo took off her shoes, she would have to step in the pool of glue and would still be stuck.

He watched as she struggled to reach a bottle on a nearby shelf—and grabbed it. Cal hoped whatever was in the bottle would help her get free, but he couldn't read the label.

He could see Leslie Wylot, though. She was sneaking out of the Hardware Circle, carrying something that looked like a fishing net. Cal swore he could make out an earbud in her ear, and her mouth was moving under her bandana. She was talking!

So that was why the Wylots had chosen costumes with bandanas that hid their faces. They were wearing headsets to communicate with each other. They must have grabbed them in the Fun and Games Circle.

Bug tugged Cal's arm and pointed to the TV that showed the Pet Circle, which looked quite pleasant. Fake tree branches tangled over the Circle, creating a home for the Butterfly of Savings. But their dad was there—and he was in big trouble. At the bottom of the screen, Cal could see Mr. Wylot opening animal cages in the Pet Circle. He was releasing all the snakes, including the giant boa constrictor.

The families weren't allowed to talk, but that didn't mean Cal couldn't communicate. A store microphone was glued to a display case of remote controls. For years, people had been saying Cal wanted to be a puppet master. Now was his chance to see if he had what it took.

Cal picked up the mike and tapped it with his palm.

BANG! The sound echoed through the overhead speakers all around the store. On the screens, the Wylots and Talaskas looked up.

Cal signaled for Butler to drop the Friendly Farmer in his mouth. Butler cocked his head as if saying, *Why?* But he did it.

Cal flipped the toy over and lifted a flap to reveal the touch screen. He pressed START and held the farmer up to the microphone.

"The sheep says . . . ," the Friendly Farmer announced. The toy paused, waiting for Cal to type in what a sheep said. Cal hit a series of letters on the touch screen.

"*Moo?*" the farmer said. "No, no, NO! That's just SILLY!"

There was a reason these toys were on sale. The

farmer sounded like an annoying know-it-all with a singsongy voice.

Cal typed more letters. "The cow says . . . *Fitness!*" the farmer blathered. "No, no, NO! That's just SILLY!"

Bug covered his ears. And Cal nearly did, too. The voice was getting on his nerves. But it was working. In the Fitness Circle, his mom looked up at the camera. Her face said, *What the Swiss is going on?*

"The chicken says . . . *Sign!*" Before the farmer could say "No, no, NO!" Cal pulled it away from the microphone. He watched as his mom thought about the message. She pointed at the sign that said THIS WAY CLOSED!, and Cal pushed buttons again. This time, the farmer proclaimed, "The goose says . . . *Wrong!*"

His mom touched the fake sign and it came loose, revealing the real sign underneath.

Cal's fingers pressed the toy again. "The rooster says . . . *Yes!*"

His mom gave a thumbs-up. She got it. She was heading the right way now.

Bug tapped the timer on the cart.

The numbers 10:23 blinked at them. Just over ten minutes left!

Cal didn't have time to go through the same thing with Imo and his dad. It would be faster if Cal, Bug, and Butler went to them.

★ ★ ★

With Bug pulling the cart behind them, Cal and Butler raced down the aisle. Cal imagined the map. He knew they had to run through the Sporting Goods Circle to reach the Hardware Circle, where Imo was stuck.

The aisle suddenly opened up into the Sporting Goods Circle—and *WHAP!* Something flew out of nowhere and struck Cal's shoulder. The force spun him back into the aisle next to Bug and Butler, but he kept his balance.

What the heck was that?

Bug picked up the foam dart that someone had fired at Cal. It was the size of a loaf of bread. Butler grabbed it in his mouth and started tearing it up.

Cal poked his head around the edge of the aisle. In the center of the Sporting Goods Circle, a display of three tennis ball–serving machines sat on a steel table. A sign read: THE ENDLESS SERVER—RETURNS TENNIS BALLS FOR HOURS!

He could just barely make out her face, but Cal could see Emma Wylot crouched on the table between two of the serving machines. She must have snagged a foam-dart gun from the Fun and Games Circle. She aimed it at Cal and fired again.

Cal ducked back into the aisle. He and Bug were safe where they were, but they couldn't get across the Circle. Cal couldn't risk Bug's getting pegged by a dart. His parents would never forgive him. They would have to go back and hope they could find a different route to the rest of the family. They could get the ribbon from this Circle later.

Even as he thought this, Cal knew they'd never have enough time.

Before they left the Circle, he couldn't resist giving Emma a piece of his mind. He poked his head out again and pointed his eyes at her. *I see you! This isn't fair!*

Emma didn't even bother to give a nasty wave, as Leslie usually did. She just shrugged.

Cal turned to pull Bug along with him when he spotted Imo on the other side of the Circle. She had freed herself from the glue pool and was jumping up and down to get his attention. Then she kicked the ground. It reminded Cal of a little kid pouting.

I know it stinks that we can't get through! Cal said by shaking his head and throwing up his hands.

No! That's not it! Imo pointed again at her kicking foot. Frustrated that Cal still wasn't getting what she meant, she turned away.

Tugging her ear, she looked at the shelves around her, and Cal could almost feel her brain buzzing. Even Emma stood up a little to see what she had planned.

In a blur of movement, Imo grabbed a ski helmet and put it on her head. She put four skateboards on the floor and laid a surfboard on top of them. She put one foot on the surfboard and pushed back and forth, back and forth, with the other. When she had enough momentum, she stood on the surfboard and shot across the Circle.

Emma had been waiting for this. She stood all the way up and raised the foam-dart gun.

The force of the dart would knock Imo off the board. And, helmet or no helmet, the fall would sting.

Emma fired—

But Imo must have been waiting for her opponent's move, too. She dropped to her knees and then lay on her back on the rolling surfboard. The dart sailed over her. Imo reached up and snagged the Talaskas' ribbon as she slid under the display table. Before Emma could reload, Imo had rolled past Cal and into the safety of his aisle.

Grinning, Imo jumped off her surfboard "lawn luge" and handed Cal her ski helmet and the ribbon. Without hesitating, she walked back to the aisle opening.

Cal reached out to pull Imo back. She shook her head and pointed at her kicking foot again and then behind Cal. He turned and finally got it. *Oh!*

A display of kickball launchers lined the shelf. They were plugged in and loaded with red rubber balls, like the ones from gym class. They were facing the center of the Circle.

Imo moved to switch them on. Once again, Emma knew what she was up to. Emma had turned the tennis ball–serving machines toward their aisle. She gave Imo a little salute. Imo returned the salute, and the two girls shared a look of grudging respect.

Then they both started switching on the different machines. The tennis balls fired across the Circle at the Talaskas, and the kickballs shot toward the center of the Circle.

As if her work here was done, Emma slung the strap of the dart gun over her shoulder and climbed off the display table. With one last look at the Talaskas, she quickly left the Circle.

Cal saw they could get across the Circle now. Each time a tennis ball fired out of a machine toward them, a flying kickball was there to block it. Just in case, he put the ski helmet on Bug. Then, with Cal and Imo leading the way, Bug pulled the cart under the colliding balls to the other side. One tennis ball was knocked free and hit Cal square in the forehead. *Smack!* Right where he'd been slapping his forehead earlier. Cal wondered if he had a bull's-eye painted there.

We did it! he said silently, and the three kids shared a high five and a quick snuggle with Butler. In a flash, Imo shoved a box she'd grabbed onto the bottom of the shopping cart.

Cal didn't take time to see what it was. They took off sprinting toward the path that ran around the entire store. Up ahead, Mrs. T. was waiting.

She was breathless, but she was standing like a relay racer ready to run a lap. She tossed her box into the cart and handed Cal the ribbon from the Fitness Circle.

Cal pointed to the timer, then toward the Pet Circle. *We don't have much time to meet Dad!*

Even though she was wearing her sweatband, sweat poured down her face. But she nodded. *Let's go!*

The timer read 7:34.

Unlike the other Circles, with their tons of aisles, the Pet Circle had only two ways in. Sliding glass doors opened and closed on their own as people entered and left. That kept the Butterfly of Savings and any of the slithery critters from escaping.

The air in the Circle was heavy and humid, as in the birdhouse at the Grand Rapids zoo. The shelves were filled with dog food, cat litter, squeaky toys, and cages and tanks of animals and bugs.

To keep from distracting shoppers, Wish Shoppe sold only creatures that didn't make much noise. There were plenty of fish, silent insects, and, of course . . . snakes.

Butler's mouth had popped open, and he was looking

around as if he were in heaven. Mrs. T. looked intently at Bug and put her hands on his shoulders. *Stay with Butler,* she mouthed.

The wide trunk of a fake tree rose out of the center, sprouting branches and leaves that wove across the ceiling. Cal knew from a security camera that his dad was stuck against the wall on the other side. They found Mr. T. there, holding a huge object wrapped in what looked like a dog blanket. Cal could see the Pet Circle's ribbon poking out of his pants pocket.

Mr. T.'s face lit up when he saw them, but he stayed frozen. Why wasn't he moving?

Mrs. T. made her *What the cheddar is going on?* face.

Mr. T.'s eyes darted around the room, as if telling his family to follow where he was looking. Cal did and discovered that the Talaskas were not alone.

All four Wylots were in the Pet Circle, too. Emma was actually on the ceiling, swinging from branch to branch, the foam-dart gun in her belt. Mr. and Mrs. Wylot were looking under crates. Leslie had the net on a pole, and she was also scouring the room for something.

What are they looking for with a net? Cal wondered. Then it hit him.

The butterfly! The Wylots were going to grab King Wonder's butterfly!

It was worth the world to King Wonder. And Cal imagined how Mr. Wylot would use that to get what he really wanted. Maybe he would demand to be part owner of Wish Shoppe and have even more people working for him.

No matter what the Wylots were up to, the timer was still ticking. The Talaskas had to get out of there.

Come on, Dad, Cal said with his eyes. Then he made squiggly motions while shaking his head. *There are no snakes. They're all hiding.*

Mr. T. shook his head. *It's not the snakes! It's this!*

Careful not to let the Wylots see, Mr. T. turned very slowly. *Holy Aristotle.* With fluttering purple wings the size of dinner plates, the biggest butterfly Cal had ever seen was perched on his dad's back.

It was King Wonder's Butterfly of Savings.

Mr. T. raised a finger to his lips and looked up. Cal understood. His dad didn't want to move because he was scared of revealing the flying insect to the Wylots.

The Talaskas needed to get the butterfly back into the branches without the Wylots' seeing it.

Mrs. T. raised her hand. *I know what to do!* She made

a typing gesture, like she was sitting in front of an invisible computer.

Cal wanted to shout, *Are you sending an invisible email?*

She held up a finger, as if she had just discovered something.

Oh! Something you found online? Cal mouthed.

Mrs. T. nodded. She hurried to the wall and reached for the light switch. The Wylots saw it and stamped their feet. Emma dropped to the ground, rushing to stop Mrs. T.

No! No! the Wylots seemed to be saying. Cal wanted to join them.

Trust me, Mrs. T.'s face said, and then she flicked the light switch.

The Pet Circle plunged into darkness.

The Wylots and Talaskas were suddenly rushing about the Circle. No one was talking—at least that

Cal could hear—but there were grunts of surprise and what sounded like a struggle.

Cal felt something slither up his leg. Being unable to talk was probably a good thing. He wasn't sure the Friendly Farmer was allowed to say what was running through his head.

Cal spun away from the spot. He felt the creature on his leg shake free and launch into the air.

Click! The light came back on. Mrs. T. put her hands together on her cheek and tilted her head as if she were sleeping, and pointed up.

Cal got it!

Mrs. T.'s research had paid off again. The butterfly thought it was nighttime and had flown to the safety of the branches to rest.

The Wylots had been on the move, too. While the room was dark, the entire family had rushed out the door that the Talaskas had used. It was sliding shut.

Just as it was about to close, Emma noticed what the Talaskas were looking at. She lifted her dart gun and aimed up at the Butterfly of Savings. Her eyes said it all. If the Wylots couldn't have the butterfly, no one could.

NO! Cal thought.

Even Leslie looked shocked. She shook her head at Emma. But Emma pulled the trigger anyway. The dart shot through the air.

Cal had a choice. He could leap forward to keep the door from shutting, or he could jump up to stop the dart.

He leapt and swatted the dart down.

The door slid shut. Through the glass, Cal saw Mr. Wylot pop Leslie's net into the outside track of the door. It was locked, with the Talaskas stuck inside the Circle.

Emma pointed out the butterfly to Mr. Wylot. His eyes lit up, and he reached to lift the net so he could open the door—

In a flash, Imo's hand shot out. She turned the lock on the inside of the door.

Now the Wylots couldn't get in, but the Talaskas still couldn't get out. They faced off in two lines on either side of the glass door.

Mr. Wylot shrugged, and Cal guessed what he was thinking. It was too bad Mr. Wylot couldn't capture the Butterfly of Savings, but he'd still show the Talaskas and the world who was boss.

Leslie held up the Wylots' ribbons and fanned them

out so Cal could count them. Nine. The Wylots had gathered all the ribbons. They just needed to get to the finish line first.

Cal spun around. At least the door on the other side of the Circle was open. For now.

Emma jerked to one side. Cal's heart bumped. Was she going to race around the outside of the Circle and get to the open door first? But she just threw back her head and laughed silently.

Leslie gave a nasty wave, and the Wylots sauntered off, pushing their empty cart, as if they had all the time in the world.

But for the Talaskas, time was running out. Their cart's timer blinked:

3:56.

It was impossible. There was no way the Talaskas could run around the store, gather the last four ribbons they needed, and beat the Wylots to the finish line.

That was when Mr. T. pulled the Pet Circle ribbon from his pocket and handed it to Cal. Something felt different about it. Cal looked down and saw he was actually holding five ribbons stacked on top of each other. That made a total of nine.

The Talaskas had all the ribbons!

How? Cal asked, stunned.

Mr. T. smiled and acted like he was studying an invisible wall. *I memorized the map. All of it!*

He must have been running all over that side of the store before going to the Pet Circle. Imo, Mrs. T., and Bug were jumping up and down. Cal didn't care if it wasted time. He gave his dad a hug.

Then Cal clapped his hands. *We have to get out of here.*

Imo nodded furiously. *Go! Go! Go!*

Mr. T. threw his wrapped bundle into the cart. It was heavy, and there was no room left in the overflowing cart. Cal didn't take the time to wonder how it had gotten so full.

Bug was pulling away like an unstoppable sled dog, with Mrs. T. pushing behind the cart. Mr. T. was running in front with Butler, and Imo and Cal ran on either side, just in case the cart tipped or something fell out.

On this side of the Pet Circle, they were in uncharted territory. Only Mr. T. knew the way, or at least Cal hoped he did. Cal was starting to worry when he spotted a big sign with an arrow:

THIS WAY TO EMPLOYEE EXIT
Employees only! All others, please use main exit!

Yes! An exit! The family picked up speed and ran in the direction of the arrow.

Fifty yards later, they slammed open the exit door and burst out of the maze into the sunshine. The non-air-conditioned breeze felt incredible. With his ears free of the store's perky music, Cal could think more clearly.

But that sound was replaced by the roar of the crowd.

The Wylots were nowhere in sight, but the spectators were a hundred feet away, still gathered on the other side of the River of Low Prices. A sidewalk ran from the store to the river. The Talaskas needed to race down that sidewalk, cross the bridge, and reach the finish line.

"No way they're going to make it in time!" a man in the crowd shouted.

"I'll bet you a dollar they give up right now," a woman shouted back. "The Wylots never lose!"

Cal wasn't the only one who heard them. Bug's head snapped up. A look of determination came over his face. He slowed down and reached out to scratch Butler behind the ears.

"What's that kid doing?" a little boy asked.

Cal knew. Bug and Butler were choosing this moment to finally perform their B&B Scooter Madness Stunt in public.

Bug took off running. Cal grabbed for his shirt, but missed as the cart whizzed away.

No, Bug!

A kid and a dog on a mission, Bug and Butler ran toward the River of Low Prices. Cal knew that Bug imagined himself sailing over the river with the cart, landing dramatically on the other side. Then the finish line would be just a short trot away.

What happened instead was a catastrophe.

Butler made a wide turn before coming to the two-foot-high concrete ledge that ran along the river, since they had always practiced avoiding the "target" at the last moment. But Bug jumped over the ledge. The cart rammed into it and didn't budge as he sailed through the air. The harness went tight and yanked Bug back, slamming him against the ledge with a *whap!*

Someone in the crowd groaned sympathetically. "Ouch!"

Bug dangled over the side in the harness, his feet submerged in the River of Low Prices.

As fast as her body would move, Mrs. T. scrambled to kneel on the ledge. She pulled the harness and hauled Bug up like a fish. He wasn't crying and hurt. He just looked angry that his stunt didn't work after all. Mrs. T. hugged him and put him down on the other side of the ledge. Butler was there immediately, nuzzling Bug worriedly.

Mrs. T. stood so she could step off the ledge, too. That was when all the running caught up with her. She started to lose her balance. For one awful moment, she tottered on the edge of the River of Low Prices.

Cal reached for her. *Mom—*

And then she slipped.

Mrs. T. spun in the air and hit the water on her belly. *Smack!* She came up on her knees, soaking wet, just her shoulders and head above the water. She had lost her headband, and her hair was matted to her face.

There was a burst of laughter from the crowd, with a few hoots and cruel jeers, as the news cameras rushed over to capture the moment.

"How's the water?" a high school kid asked.

Mrs. T. didn't seem able to move. In fact, none of the Talaskas did.

Except Imo.

With a nod to Cal, she took a step forward, and Cal could almost hear the cameras zooming in on her. The attention would normally make her shy, but not now. Imo climbed on top of the ledge so everyone could see her. She raised her eyes and her head, and then in a loud, clear voice, she said, "*In my opinion,* you're a winner, Mom."

Imo jumped down into the waist-high water. She fished around for something near her feet. It was the headband, and she tossed it to her mom. Mrs. T. pushed her hair back and put the wet headband around her head.

Her eyes were shiny as she mouthed, *Thank you, Imo.*

"No problem," Imo said, helping Mrs. T. out of the river. "And we only have eighteen seconds."

Cal's gaze went to the timer. It was true. Now just seventeen seconds. Make that sixteen. Fifteen.

In a flash, Cal thought of all the things he could say to convince his family they could do this. They *could* reach the finish line on time. All the bottled-up words from the past twenty minutes wanted to pour out at once.

Cal opened his mouth and this came out:

"Ahhhhhhh!"

It felt so good to yell after being silent for so long that Cal didn't think he could stop.

And he wasn't alone. Soon his whole family was shouting and barking. They raced toward the finish line, suddenly the world's loudest family.

"AHHHHHHH!"

Just then, the Wylots came out of the main entrance. They had ditched the bandanas and the headsets. And they were taking their time, as if winning the contest were the easiest thing in the world.

"Hurry, Mr. Wylot!" Alison's dad shouted. "They're coming!"

The Wylots spotted the Talaskas. It was as if a giant, invisible hand goosed all the Wylots. They leapt in the air, and then they were off and running.

The Talaskas' stuffed cart was shaking so hard, Cal

thought it would collapse. Mrs. T. was managing to keep up, but her wheezing was getting much worse.

The two families reached the bridge at the same time. The carts slammed into each other like chariots in an action movie, and the wheels bumped and collided. The Wylots shoved and pushed, and the Talaskas struggled to keep their cart upright.

The crowd counted down the last seconds.

"Three!"

The families raced across the bridge.

"Two!"

They were just a few feet from the finish line.

"One!"

The crowd roared. The Talaskas and the Wylots—
and their carts—had all crossed the finish line in
time.

"It's a tie!" an old woman shrieked.

Exhausted, the Talaskas fell on top of each other in
front of King Wonder's throne. Once again, they were a
rolling ball of arms, legs, a tail, and giggling. Cal felt as
hysterical as he'd been while making the video weeks ago.

"Don't find the missing *P*, Cal!" Coach Eaton yelled.

Cal just laughed. When he looked up, he found the
Wylots standing in a line watching them and laughing,
too.

"Congratulations, Wylots! Looks like we're all winners!" Mrs. T. said. The Talaskas climbed to their feet,

and their hysteria died down to chuckles. But the Wylots kept laughing. Even the normally silent Emma was guffawing like crazy. It was creepy, and Mrs. T. asked uncertainly, "Pretty funny that we're all winners, right?"

"Oh, that's not why we're so happy," Mr. Wylot said. "We're not laughing *with* you. We're laughing *at* you."

Leslie grinned at Cal, then pointed at Imo. "You broke the rules, *Jessie*," Leslie announced with glee. "We weren't allowed to talk during the contest. But you said, 'In my opinion, you're a winner, Mom.' We're the winners. Not bragging. Google it."

The Wylots must have been listening in on their headsets just before they tossed them.

"What this little girl did was very, very sweet," Mr. Wylot said, gesturing at Imo. "But a clear violation of the rules. Don't you think, King?"

King Wonder hesitated. Mr. Wylot cleared his throat loudly twice until Mr. Vance met his gaze. Mr. Wylot made a signal with his hand. Mr. Vance ducked his head to whisper to King, who nodded as he listened.

"The Wylots are correct," King said. "The Talaskas must be disqualified."

No! Cal thought. *Imo managed to stop being shy, and now this? Has her bravery cost us the contest?*

King held out his hands as if there were nothing else he could do. "We are going to declare the winning family to be—" he started to say.

"Wait?" a voice shouted. It was Sarah!

Bug's babysitter was rushing through the crowd toward them.

"You can't let the Wylots win this time?" Sarah said to King when she reached the Talaskas.

Mrs. T. touched Sarah's arm. "Thanks, sweetie," Cal's mom said, and then lowered her voice. "But remember, Mr. Wylot controls the money you need for school. He could take it away from you."

"It's not much of an education if it keeps me from doing what's right?" Sarah responded.

"Here's a little education for *you*," Mr. Wylot said to the Talaskas. "Even with nothing in our cart or if we barely try, the Wylots will always beat you. We'll always win."

This was too much for Mr. T. "I . . . I . . . ," he said.

"Oh, this should be good," Mr. Wylot said. He looked like a cat about to toy with a mouse. "Come on, Nelson.

Use your words. Maybe a rhyme about being jobless and having a family you can't feed?"

At the mention of *family*, Mr. T.'s face changed. His eyes narrowed and he stood up straighter. "This is wrong, Mr. Wylot," he said, "and you know it."

"Dad, that doesn't rhyme," Cal said.

"Because I'm not nervous," Mr. T. said. "Because I'm right."

Mr. Wylot shot a look at Mr. Vance, who whispered into King's ear again. When he pulled back, King frowned and said, "We need to declare the winner. And, well, we—"

"Please, can I say something?" Cal asked.

King nodded absently, and Cal stepped forward. This was going to take all his skill. At the front of the crowd, Ms. Graves nodded at him. "Go for it, Cal," she told him quietly. "Talk him over to your side!"

But Cal had figured out something while running around the store. He didn't always need to talk. Sometimes it was just all about listening.

He took a breath and said to King, "Excuse me, sir, but didn't you say there was no talking *inside* the store?"

"My goodness, the boy is right!" James called,

copying the mayor's voice. Then, in Leslie's voice, he said, "Why, I think he might be onto something!"

Leslie clapped a hand over her mouth as if words were escaping her lips.

Ms. Donegan nodded. "Cal's right. King did say that." A few people murmured, as if they remembered the same thing.

"When my sister spoke, she was *outside* the store," Cal said.

Mr. Wylot snapped his fingers angrily at Mr. Vance, who leaned toward King Wonder's ear again. This time, though, King held up a hand to block him.

"You know," King said, "we like it when people *listen* to us." He gave Mr. Vance a look. "And when they aren't always *telling* us what to do."

King's eyes went from Mr. Vance to the Wylots' empty cart and their angry faces and, finally, to Cal. He seemed to like what he saw, and he nodded.

Turning to the cameras, King said, "The Tal . . . Tal . . . this family is correct. The ban against talking was only inside the store. We declare a tie! Both families are winners!"

The crowd cheered, mostly fueled by Sarah and the

Talaskas' friends. Alison joined in the clapping. Her dad instantly pulled her away, toward their car. She gave Cal a last smile over her shoulder.

Leslie's braids were shaking with anger. "How can we both be winners?" she asked her dad. "Does that mean the Talaskas are our equals?"

"Bite your tongue!" Mr. Wylot snapped.

"Not to worry, my friends," King Wonder told the Wylots. "Both families are winners. They can keep whatever is inside their carts."

"But there's nothing in our cart!" Leslie said. "All we have are these ribbons!"

"Oh, we see," King Wonder said, as if trying to keep a straight face. "Too bad. We guess we were wrong about the *winners* part." He rose from the throne and walked to the Talaskas' overflowing cart. "This cart tells a different story, though, doesn't it?"

Now that King Wonder was standing closer, Cal saw how red his cheeks were and how excited he was about the contest. "Let's see what we have here," he said, like a little kid about to unwrap a present. "What did you grab for yourself, Mrs. Tal . . . Tallulah . . . ?"

Cal's mom smiled. "It's Talaska. But Mrs. T. is fine."

He smiled back. "Well, what did you get for yourself, Mrs. T.?"

"Oh, we all know," Mr. Wylot said. "She got herself home gym equipment. The rest of them grabbed a keyboard, a laboratory, a video game system, and . . . that one?" He pointed at Bug. "I don't know, candy or something. Their cart might as well be filled with nothing, too."

Cal couldn't believe it. Mr. Wylot remembered everything Cal had said the Talaskas wanted on the day of the first elimination.

"I'd like to show you what we got, Mr. Wonder," Mrs. T. said. She took out the small box she had grabbed. "I don't know why this was in the Fitness Circle, but I do know where it will find a good home. It's for you, honey."

Mrs. T. gave the box to a surprised Imo.

"But what about something for your home gym?" Imo asked. "Or something for your trivia?"

"I'll get the trivia organized later," Mrs. T. said. "Right now, I want to work on the big stuff."

Imo opened the box and removed a smaller one, shiny silver and about half the size of a toaster. She put it down and flicked a switch on the side. *BLAM!* A

parachute fired out of the box, creating a kind of ceiling over the family. Light shot up from the box and reflected off the parachute, filling the surface over their heads with stars, planets, moons, and zipping comets.

The crowd oohed and aahed.

"It's a mobile planetarium, which normally only museums can afford," Mrs. T. said. "Now you can start planning trips for the spacecraft you're going to invent."

Imo tugged her earlobe as her eyes wandered across the stars above, and then she smiled at Mrs. T. "Thanks, Mom," she said. "I got something for you, too."

It took both hands, but she pulled a large plastic bundle out of the box she had picked up at the Sporting Goods Circle. She put it at Mrs. T.'s feet and said, "It's a giant inflatable pool. Not quite a home gym, but it's a start."

"I love it," Mrs. T. said. "Thanks, honey."

King Wonder, giddy, was clapping. "And, Cal, what about you?" he asked. "What did you get? My Wonder World Video Game System?"

Cal nodded. "For a second," he said. "But then I decided on this." He reached into the cart and pulled out the box he had grabbed in the Fun and Games Circle. He gave it to his dad.

"I knew you wouldn't get something for yourself, Dad," Cal said. "You can finally put that talent for music and words to good use."

It was a sound-effects keyboard. Instead of notes, the keys produced *BLURP, SPLOOSH, SPLAT*, and *PFFFFT*.

Mr. T. laughed. He handed Cal a box from the Music Circle. Inside were a mallet and a gong that was as tall as Bug. "It can replace the small bell at home," Mr. T. explained. "Use it to call family meetings whenever you have another big idea."

"Oh, that's . . . awesome," Cal said. "Thanks, Dad." Actually, he wasn't sure what to make of the gift.

"What?" Mr. T. asked. "You don't like it?"

"No, I'm sorry," Cal said. "Sure I do."

Mr. T. said, "You know, all those years as an accountant rubbed off on me. That mallet is pure gold and probably the most expensive thing in the store!"

Cal liked the sound of that and gave the gong a whack with his hand. *ZWONG!*

"If you decide to sell the mallet," Mr. T. said, "it won't solve all our problems. But it will pay the bills for a couple of months—and give us some time to figure out our next step as a family. Maybe even help Sarah with school if she needs it."

"Amazing," Cal said. "But what about Bug?"

"Rabbo," Bug said to Butler. And then he added, "Don't worry about me, Cal."

KA-BLAM! The words were like a lightning bolt. Cal was stunned. His little brother had just said real words!

Cal could tell that his dad was trying to keep calm, as if he didn't want to scare Bug into only barking again. Mr. T. gave Bug a high five.

"This is what I really wanted!" Bug said, pointing at his family around him. "But I got other stuff, too."

Bug started pulling things out of the cart. Most of them had probably been buried under the other boxes, unless Cal had been too distracted to notice.

There was a napkin dispenser from the café, a

doorstopper from the entrance of the store, a robotic beaver from the River of Low Prices, a Friendly Farmer, a plastic *B* from a sign inside the Wish Shoppe, and a huge dog bone for Butler.

"Rabbo!" Butler barked, and ran circles around Bug.

Cal had to admit that it was a pretty good haul. And Bug wasn't done yet. He held out a foot-long screw.

Crash! Something fell inside the store.

King Wonder cringed, then laughed. "Are the winners ready for their picture?"

"Will it appear all over the country?" Imo asked.

King nodded. "Yes, young lady, it will."

"Good," Imo said. "I want everyone to see what a perfect family we have."

Cal couldn't have said it better himself.

Mrs. T. reached over to hug Imo. The cord of her inflatable pool got tangled around her ankle. In an explosion of air, the pool inflated.

At that instant, a photographer snapped the family's picture for the Wish Shoppe ad campaign.

Cal could imagine what the photo would show: Mr. T. standing behind the sound-effects keyboard, Bug holding up the *B*, Cal banging the gong—with the whole family in the inflatable pool under the planetarium's stars,

next to the grinning King Wonder. In the background, Cal dreamed, people could see the Rivales stacked in a crazy human pyramid as the Wylots slinked off to their limo.

The cameras zoomed in on the Talaskas. Imo was too excited to be nervous as she answered reporters' questions. "Well, first," she said straight into a camera, "I want to say hi to Grandma Gigi. In my opinion, she should be here with us."

Cal felt the weight of the mallet in his hand. He

couldn't wait to try it out on the new family-bell gong thing.

He hadn't told his family about the other contests he'd been checking out. He had his eye on one at an amusement park. But from the loopy grins on their faces, Cal didn't think he would need to scheme too much to convince them to enter.

After all, they were now the Prizewinners of Piedmont Place.

Is your house falling down?
Time to call in the Head Clown!

FUNLAND FUN HOUSE MAKEOVER CONTEST

Want a slide to the outside, a bumper-car kitchen—
or maybe a trampoline bed?
Our clown squad will turn your old
home into a new fun house!

PLUS: Your town will WIN $10,000!

The contest will run each month until
we have a winning family. . . . ENTER NOW!

FUNLAND AMUSEMENT PARK
We can't wait to make you LIKE us!